FIRST VOYAGE

THE SEA LORD
⚓CHRONICLES⚓
BOOK ONE

To Marilyn,
Enjoy the voyage!

DAVID HEALEY

INTRACOASTAL

Cover art by Nick Deligaris

BISAC Subject Headings:

FIC009030 FICTION/Fantasy/Historical

FIC032000 FICTION/War & Military

FIC047000 FICTION/Sea Stories

ISBN:0615733344
ISBN:978-0615733340

Dedicated to my own crew of *Formstones*,
along with many friends and advance readers
for putting wind in the tale and tending the lines.

CHAPTER 1

It was not a promising day for Alexander Hope to begin his career at sea. Snow had fallen during the night, leaving the wharves at Spithead Harbor blanketed in white. Cold had swooped in from the distant steppes of Russia, making the air so crisp that iron turned brittle and rang like crystal. The stevedores loading the ships for the war against the Emperor Napoleon Bonaparte stamped their feet in the snow and muttered about the whims of admirals and kings.

Out where the fleet lay at anchor, some beast roared and the sound seemed amplified in the arctic air. He wondered if it might actually be a gryphon. Alexander's heart skipped a beat and he shivered, not just from the cold.

"Quit your daydreaming and watch out!"

growled a man carrying a heavy sack over his shoulder.

Alexander dodged out of the way. Otherwise, no one paid any attention to the boy staring out at the harbor. The smell of salt was so sharp that it stung Alexander's nose after the warmth of the tavern where he had spent the night— along with the last shilling allotted him by his tight-fisted uncle, a man so penny-pinching that he sometimes dried out his tea leaves to use them again.

His new Royal Navy uniform and heavy wool cloak—another grudging investment from his uncle—felt stiff, but he was glad for the added warmth this morning. The cloak was secured with a beautiful silver cloak pin in the shape of a sea horse. He was surprised when one of the servants had given it to him, explaining that it was a Hope family heirloom.

"This ought to be yours, seeing as to how you're going to sea," the old man had said. "A lot of good it will do your uncle. But it will bring you luck. And kindly don't tell your uncle I gave it to you."

He touched the cloak pin now, hoping for some of that luck. But as he stared at the frozen harbor, Alexander had never felt so utterly alone. Days of traveling by himself and sleeping in strange taverns among rough men had jangled his nerves. He knew he should be excited about going to sea, but he felt instead that his life had somehow come to an ending rather than a new beginning. He already missed the empty, rambling rooms of his uncle's country house and the wide open fields he explored every summer. But there was no turning back now.

"You there, get in the boat!"

Certain that whoever had shouted must have meant *him*, Alexander looked down to see a skiff containing three sailors, obviously as miserable as he was from the cold. They glared up at him with surly expressions.

"Are you from the *Resolution*?" Alexander asked. He had meant for his voice to sound strong and confident, but it had come out weak and stuttering from his shivering lips.

"No, lad, we're from the bloody moon," the biggest of the sailors grumped. "Now get in the boat before we all freeze to death or get crushed in this ice."

He saw that the sailors had cracked the ice with their oars to get in close to the wharf, but there was enough of a swell off the harbor to make the small skiff bounce and bob like a bit of fruit in a punch bowl. Alexander's stomach promptly mimicked the motion of the boat. He had been raised among woods and country fields, and the sea was alien and strange. The spark and glitter of morning sun off the choppy open water hurt his eyes.

"It won't tip, will it?" Alexander asked, looking with not a little trepidation at the uninvitingly cold and icy water. He regretted asking the question the moment it left his mouth as the sailors exchanged an incredulous look.

"The ship is set to sail on the tide, young master, and the captain is waiting for you. If you make the captain miss the tide, I wouldn't give a brass farthing for your chances on the *Resolution*. The captain will have my hide, and then I'll have yours, ensign or not! Now scurry down that ladder there and get in the boat, if you please!"

Alexander needed no further encouragement. He struggled to lift his oak-bound sea chest and handed it down awkwardly to the man in the boat. He saw now that the man was quite large and took the sea chest as if it weighed no more than a hat box. The sailor settled it in the bottom of the skiff with a thump.

As he started to descend the ladder, Alexander felt weighed down by his new coat and numb from the cold. He had no gloves—his uncle was far too miserly to waste money on something so luxurious as gloves—and so Alexander's hands going down the ladder to the skiff were like frozen claws.

"Sit down, sit down there at the bow, or you'll have us all in the drink!" commanded the sailor.

"Which way is the bow?" Alexander was forced to ask.

"Neptune save us," the sailor said with an exaggerated eye roll, clearly disgusted. "If this is what we're being sent these days to man our ships, we'll all be speaking French within the year." He jerked his chin toward the front of the skiff.

Alexander settled there, feeling miserable, cold, and not a little seasick already. It occurred to him that the sailors should have been addressing him with a bit more deference, considering that an ensign was—technically speaking—an officer. But at the moment he was not in a position to argue the point.

"Twenty years at sea and I'm wet nurse to a land-lubber," the sailor muttered. The man's hands were so large that the oars appeared thin as broomsticks as he gripped them. His companions at the oars grinned.

"That's the King's Navy for you, Jameson," said one of the other men. "We'd best get a move on or the captain really will have our hides for jib sails. We're late enough as it is."

Alexander shrugged deeper into his enormous greatcoat, hoping he might disappear into it altogether. He supposed he should feel this was the start of a great adventure and a new life as an officer in the Royal Navy, but he only felt inconsequential—and slightly scared. He was not a little boy, but neither was he a man—at least not in the way that these burly, scruffy-faced sailors were. No, he was something in between, and the thought made him uneasy.

He looked out beyond Spithead Harbor at the gray ocean waves and tried to summon every scrap of bravery within him, but it felt a bit like shaking an empty cup. The truth was that he had never felt so alone. He had a wild thought of throwing himself into the cold sea and swimming back to shore. But he knew that nothing awaited him there.

His uncle certainly would not welcome him back because he had treated Alexander's departure with an ill-concealed pleasure, saying, "Goodbye, nephew" in a manner that had a ring of finality to it. No, his future lay with the sea and the Royal Navy, and he would just have to make the best of it.

As the sailors rowed, broken sea ice slushed against the sides of the wooden skiff. An offshore wind cut at his exposed face like a cold blade. None of the sailors seemed interested in further conversation as they concentrated on working the oars. It was probably just Alexander's imagination, but the chill water seemed thick and syrupy as the oars dipped and flashed in the winter sun. Alexander felt even more ill as the shore fell farther away.

"Still in the harbor and he's looking a bit green about the gills!" the big sailor muttered to his companions, who glanced at Alexander and grinned.

Alexander glared at them. Jameson considered himself a good judge of men and boys after years at sea, and there was a fierceness in this lad he hadn't noticed before. The boy had hollow cheeks and wild dark hair, but it was his eyes that caught Jameson's attention. They were hard and dark gray, like two stones wet by the sea. Given a little power and authority, a lad with eyes like that could be determined and strong, or he could be cruel. The sailor looked away, wondering what sort of officer this boy might become.

Slumped in the belly of the skiff, Alexander thought back to how all this had come about. It had not been his choice to go to sea, but his uncle had decided that fourteen was a good age to start on the path of a suitable career.

"A young man must make his own way in the world," his uncle had sniffed, adjusting his dingy and well-worn cravat. "I promised your father I would provide for you, and so I shall. I have found you a position in the Royal Navy. I sent a letter to an old friend of the family's, a Captain Bellingham, and he has kindly agreed to take you into service of king and country aboard his ship. It is most generous of him."

Alexander was sure he had never heard anyone mention Captain Bellingham. Not that he put much thought into recollecting the name. He was still reeling from the idea of going to sea.

His uncle had continued: "How very fortunate that a boy such as you—without prospects or promise, I might add—should be given such a position."

"The Royal Navy?" Alexander had sputtered. The thought of a life at sea was so strange that his uncle may as well have told him that he was about to be turned into a badger, or that he was being sent to a tea plantation in China. "I've never even been swimming in the ocean!"

"Then you should endeavor to say out of the water," his uncle had concluded, then stalked away to poke at the little coal fire that struggled in vain to heat the entire feudal hall at Kingston.

Alexander's family had once been rich and important, descended from Sir Algernon Hope, a powerful sea elemental who had almost single-handedly saved England from the Spanish Armada two hundred years before by conjuring a storm that wrecked the enemy fleet. Since then, his ancestors had never risen to become earls or barons or anything terribly illustrious. However, many had been officers who proudly served the king.

Whenever Alexander asked about his famous ancestor, his uncle waved off the subject.

"Don't fill your head with stories, boy! There's no such power in your veins. That was a different branch of the family altogether, and it was a long, long time ago. An elemental, indeed! Ha! Now, lad, go fetch some coal for the fire. Just a lump or two will do, mind you. Coal costs money!"

Alexander was too used to doing chores to complain, but lugging the coal from the cellar was simply another reminder that a proper gentleman would have servants to fetch the coal and stoke the fire. Instead, his uncle had him.

His uncle owned a country estate that was mostly overgrown and weedy, but the woods and fields made an excellent place for a boy to roam and daydream. The ancestral home, known as Kingston Hall, was cold and drafty, with rooms that had been closed off and furniture covered with tarps or sheets. His uncle had sold the more valuable pieces and even the swords and shields that had once covered the walls.

All in all, his uncle's home was an empty, cold place where one's footsteps tended to echo in the halls and stairs. Aside from a couple of ancient servants too old to work elsewhere—and too frail to carry coal up the stairs—they lived alone.

But it hadn't always been that way. Alexander could dimly recall when his father lived there with them. There had been laughter then, and roaring fires in the hearth. That had been a long time ago, on the dim edge of memory, and Alexander had shut away most of those recollections, much like the forgotten rooms at Kingston Hall.

His uncle had made Alexander's new career

known to him scarcely a month before, hardly time enough to have a uniform made, and now Alexander found himself utterly miserable in the belly of this rowboat in Spithead Harbor. The air stank of fish. His stomach churned.

"There she is, boy!" the big sailor named Jameson announced, rousing Alexander from his wallow of self pity and uncertainty. The man's voice had a tone of awe mixed with fondness. "There's the *Resolution*!"

When his uncle had said that Captain Bellingham was a friend of the family's—meaning a friend of his uncle's—Alexander had fully expected to find himself aboard a garbage scow. His treatment at the hands of the three sailors had done nothing to dissuade him of that notion. But the ship that he saw now took his breath away.

H.M.S. *Resolution* rose a full two stories above the harbor, its massive oak sides resembling a floating fortress. Gun ports lined the sides with cannons peering out like watchful eyes. The masts reached yet higher, seeming to pierce the heavens. From the topmost mast fluttered the British flag; its red, white and blue stood out brilliantly against the winter sky. Impossibly, or so it seemed to Alexander, men and boys worked high up in the rigging.

"What kind of ship is it?" he asked.

"Ha, he is a newbie, ain't he, boys!" Jameson

said with a laugh. But his voice was proud as he explained: "You are looking at a Royal Navy frigate, thirty-two guns, sixth rate, eight hundred tons, two hundred men, gryphon squadron. In other words, enough men, devil-beaks and firepower to strike proper fear in the heart of the Napoleonists."

As Alexander watched, the crew unfurled a massive sail. The wind filled the canvas, and the *Resolution* began to stir in the water like some sleepy giant brought to life.

"Just in time, boy," the big sailor said. "I'll wager you wouldn't want this ship to sail without you. Or maybe you would? Ha!"

With a few final pulls of the oars, they let the skiff glide against the *Resolution*. Beside the massive bulk of the ship, the skiff seemed no larger or sturdier than a floating leaf. The three sailors sprang into action, grabbing Alexander's new sea chest and fastening it to a line. No sooner had the knot been tied than the chest was hoisted away.

Alexander looked up and caught sight of a winged shape circling high above the rigging. He blinked, just to make sure his eyes weren't playing tricks on him.

"What's that?" he asked, pointing at the winged creature.

"Ain't you never seen a gryphon?" The big sailor shook his head. "Nasty creatures. Never will get used to the sight of 'em. Now, up you go. Can you climb the ladder, lad, or shall we have you hauled up like your luggage?"

"I can manage," Alexander answered after a moment, distracted by the sight of the soaring gryphon. He had heard of these creatures, of course, and of how they were used in defense of the realm, but he had never actually seen one. The flying beast was large as a horse, had a tawny yellow hide, a tail and feathered wings that caught the eddies of sea wind as it circled high above the ship. To Alexander's astonishment, a rider sat astride the gryphon, perched on a saddle strapped between the beating wings.

The big sailor gave him a slight push, and Alexander grabbed hold of the rope ladder and began to climb. It was harder than he had expected. His hands were stiff with cold and the heavy sea cloak seemed to weigh him down and dull his movements. The ship swayed with motion as it got underway and the sudden movement made Alexander realize how easily he might have pitched into the icy waters below.

Scaling the tall oak sides was a bit like going up a mountain. His heart hammered in his chest, but he forced himself to climb. This was his new career. He was an ensign in the Royal Navy now, not a land-lubber anymore. Besides, he wasn't about to give those surly sailors in the skiff the satisfaction of calling for help. With a final burst of energy and willpower, he reached the gunwale and climbed aboard *Resolution*.

Another boy in the uniform of an ensign had been watching his progress. He took Alexander's hand and helped him step onto the deck.

"Welcome to the *Resolution*," the boy said. "I'm Roger Higson."

Alexander took a few unsteady steps. His legs felt rubbery.

"Takes some getting used to," Roger said with a laugh. "You'll get your sea legs soon enough and then you'll walk funny when you get back on land again."

"If you say so." Alexander already felt queasy from the motion of the ship. He was in no mood to argue, but would have agreed with Roger if the boy had claimed that Alexander had two heads.

"Oh, I do," Roger said. "Now, let's get you squared away. Jameson!" The sudden shout made Alexander jump. "Take Mr. Hope's sea chest below."

The sailor gave the ensign a nod—a bit grudgingly, Alexander thought—and then hefted the chest. It was strange to see a boy ordering around a big sailor like Jameson, but Alexander reminded himself that this was the Royal Navy, a place with its own rules.

Roger turned back to him and said, "Now, let's give you a tour of the ship, gryphons and all."

CHAPTER 2

"Look lively, snotty!"

Alexander heard the shout, and just had time to throw himself to the deck as a pair of giant claws raked the air overhead. He heard the beat of massive wings and the snap of a beak. He looked up to see that Roger hadn't so much as ducked. Around him, the sailors were laughing at the new ensign who now lay sprawled among the coiled lines, his fancy new bi-corn hat tumbling away in the sea breeze. Roger grabbed it up and handed it back as Alexander regained his feet.

"What was that?"

"Gryphon." Roger shrugged. "Don't worry, you'll get used to them."

"Do they always swoop about the deck like that?" The gryphon made another sweep overhead, dodging among the masts, and as Alexander ducked again he heard the boy in the beast's saddle laughing wildly.

"Flyers," muttered Roger. "They're a disorderly lot. They can't resist making a fool out of an honest sailor. They have this idea that they are somehow superior."

Feeling a bit safer now, if somewhat foolish, Alexander had time to study the gryphon more closely. The hindquarters were those of a lion and covered in tawny fur. Up front, the beast resembled a giant eagle with brilliant brown-gold feathers. Its wings must have been twenty-five feet across. The beast was big as a draft horse, with a fearsome beak and talons like grappling hooks. But it was the eyes he noticed most of all. They were a bright, cat-like yellow.

"Hey, snotty!" the flyer called down to him.

Alexander glared at the rider, a boy his own age with pale blond hair who flew the gryphon with obvious joy. He felt the difference in their situations keenly, considering he felt anything but happiness as the ship rolled beneath his feet. The flyer waved, the gryphon tipped its wings, and they flew off.

"The first thing you must do whenever you come aboard a ship is report to the officer of the watch," Roger said, starting off down the deck. "That would be Lieutenant Swann."

Roger led them to a knot of officers who seemed to be in charge of the preparations for getting underway, calling out orders and pointing out tasks for individual sailors. In the midst of this knot stood the lieutenant, a tall young man with a sharply hooked nose.

"It's our new ensign, sir." Roger nudged him forward.

The lieutenant paused in his orders long enough to look Alexander over from head to toe. His face, however, was inscrutable.

"Mr. Hope reporting, sir." Alexander stammered, and then managed an awkward salute.

"Very good, Mr. Hope," Lieutenant Swann said. "Welcome to the *Resolution*. I see you've already met Mr. Higson ... and one of our gryphons."

"Yes, sir." Alexander felt himself go red. The lieutenant must have noticed his not-very-brave dive to the deck.

"As you can see, Mr. Hope, we are very busy getting underway with the tide. A ship this size needs to ride the outgoing tide to sea because we can't hoist much sail in the harbor. That's your first lesson in seamanship. Meanwhile, Mr. Higson here will get you acquainted with the *Resolution*."

"Thank you, sir." But the lieutenant had already turned his attention to another task at hand.

"Come on, then," Roger said cheerfully, taking Alexander by the elbow. The other ensign always seemed to have a ready smile.

"Don't we have to help with the ship?"

"Oh, there will be time for that, believe me. Besides, what good can you possibly do without knowing at least a little about the ship? So come along."

"Aye, aye." Alexander found himself smiling, and realized it was the first time he had done so in days. His face actually felt sore from the effort, as if the muscles were out of practice.

The ship was already getting underway. Only a few patches of sail had been lowered, and Alexander puzzled over that until he realized the lieutenant had said it was the tide moving the ship. Alexander couldn't quite get used to the idea that the solid-looking wooden deck beneath his feet was anything but secure as the whole ship rocked gently in the swell off the English Channel.

"Boat to stern!" someone cried.

Alexander followed the gazes of the sailors, who seemed in some consternation and excitement about the tiny sailing dingy that was overtaking them. Someone half-stood in the bow, waving his arms and shouting. "Ahoy the ship!"

A ladder was lowered, and a very flustered civilian came aboard. He was tall and gangly, dressed in a well-made but worn brown suit.

"Who's that?" Alexander wondered.

"Must be the ensigns' tutor. Another minute or two and that little sailing dingy never would have caught the *Resolution*. We'd have had had no teacher then. Lucky for him, not so lucky for us!"

As the two boys moved about the deck, Alexander cast one watchful eye skyward, but there was no sign of the gryphon.

"Why did that flyer call me 'snotty?'" Alexander asked.

"Oh, that's just a nickname for ensigns in general," Roger replied. "You see, the younger ones are always wiping their noses on their sleeves. That makes you a snotty. Get it?"

"Indeed." Silently, Alexander vowed that he would always use a proper handkerchief. He really didn't care to be called a snotty.

"The problem with being an ensign is that one doesn't always get much in the way of proper respect. Most of the hands are grown men, and it's only natural to resent being told what to do by someone younger. But you can't show them any weakness or allow them to show you disrespect or you'll never be any kind of ship's officer."

"All right." Alexander thought about how the big sailor in the skiff had treated him. The man had made no secret of the fact that he didn't think much of ensigns. Worse yet, Alexander realized, he had let him get away with it.

"The officers are of mixed opinion when it comes to ensigns," Roger went on. "You see, they tend to think of themselves as having been perfect when they were our age and officers in training, so they view ensigns with a certain amount of ... what would be the best way to phrase it—"

For some reason, Alexander thought of the expression that frequently crossed his uncle's face whenever he was lecturing him. "Disgust?"

"Exactly." Roger grinned. "You catch on fast, don't you?"

"Lieutenant Swann seems like a good man."

"Aye, one of the best. He has more patience than most for ensigns. He'll even try to teach you a thing or two when there's time."

"What about Captain Bellingham?"

Roger stopped in his tracks. "Do you believe in God?" he asked in a hushed voice.

"Why, of course I do."

"The best way I can explain the captain is this: God may rule Heaven, but Captain Bellingham rules the *Resolution*. Let's just say you don't want to do anything foolish so that you end up meeting God or the Captain any sooner than necessary. Now come on, let me give you a proper tour."

Roger disappeared down a hatch, and Alexander followed. He had never been on a ship before, and to his surprise, instead of stairs going down there was a kind of ladder. Roger went down it in an instant as easily as if the narrow ladder had been a grand staircase, but Alexander stopped, turned around, and went hand over hand, one foot and one rung at a time. When he got to the bottom, Roger was standing there, laughing.

"You are a proper land-lubber, aren't you!"

Before Alexander could answer, the other ensign darted away. The deck here was wide and spacious, but not especially high. Alexander could easily reach up and touch the ceiling. The entire deck was lined with massive cannons, each with a barrel longer than a man. The hatches over the gun ports were closed, which shut out the light and made the interior of the deck dark and gloomy, but the hatches were ill-fitting enough to let in the winter cold. Alexander could hear the winter wind whistling and tugging at the gaps. The air here smelled dank and damp like seawater and gun powder and stale sweat, but also, somehow, a bit like a barn.

"Twenty-eight guns, in case you haven't counted," Roger announced. "That's not counting the smaller guns on the deck itself."

Alexander noticed sea chests between the cannons, but the way they were decorated with stencils and actual artwork made him think that they were not for storing ammunition. Then he noticed that a few hammocks were slung between the guns. He looked more closely, and saw that men were slumbering in one or two of the hammocks. Blood-red uniforms were hung here and there on hooks.

"The marines sleep in here when they're not on watch," Roger whispered, seeing that Alexander had noticed the hammocks. "A word to the wise is that the marines keep to themselves. This section of the deck is their territory—when we don't need the guns to fight a battle."

"Why are there marines on the ship?"

"Oh, they're handy for boarding ships and amphibious landings," Roger said. He lowered his voice again. "Also, nobody likes to talk about it, but the marines are here to protect the officers and the ship if there's a mutiny, so you can understand why they don't mix much with the sailors."

"Mutiny?" Alexander's head reeled all over again. What had he gotten himself into?

"Oh, don't worry about that. It hasn't happened in a while, and Captain Bellingham is not the sort to inspire mutiny. Come on."

They crossed to the far end of the gun deck, where there was a large iron door, almost like he might have expected to see in a prison.

"Is that the brig?" he asked. He had heard about such things, where mutineers and the like were kept.

Roger laughed. "Only if you're really, really bad. Then I suppose the captain might have you fed to one of these creatures."

Before Alexander could ask the next logical question—what creatures?—he heard a noise coming from the caged area. It was somewhere between a growl and a hawk-like shriek—hard to describe exactly, except that it was a beastly noise.

"What was that?"

"Gryphon," Roger said. "Sounds hungry, doesn't it? You should see these things at feeding time. Quite ghastly, really."

Alexander stared through the barred doorway, straining to catch a glimpse of the gryphon. There were lanterns, but the gloom below decks was so thick that it was hard to make out anything definite. However, he could definitely tell that there were beastly shapes on the other side of the door. He was suddenly quite glad for the iron gate separating them. He just hoped that the bars were quite thick enough.

"Are the marines here to protect the gryphons as well?"

Roger laughed at that. "Once you've seen one of these devil-beaks up close, you'll realize that they don't need much help from the marines when it comes to protection. You wouldn't, either, if you had claws like bayonets and a beak sharp as a scythe."

As they watched, two crewmen wearing flyer uniforms went past. "Here to see the devil-beaks?" one of the men asked. "Come on through the gate if you please, young sirs."

Alexander might have thought better of it, but Roger accepted the invitation with a grin. One of the men closed and locked the gate behind them. "They've been fed today, but it's a precaution. The marines have been known to get touchy about the gate being left open, you see. They worry about the devil-beaks getting loose."

Alexander gulped back his fear. Roger didn't seem particularly afraid, so he wouldn't be, either. The two flyer crewmen set to work winding a windlass that lowered a section of the ship's side, like a drawbridge. The platform jutted into empty air and Alexander was mystified at first. He took a step closer, wondering what was out there, but all he could glimpse was sea and sky. Cold winter wind blew in.

"That's the gryphon port," Roger explained, as if reading his thoughts.

"Sir, I'd stand back if I were you," one of the flyer crew said.

Alexander had barely moved out of the way when there was a beating of wings and a screech, and then something landed heavily on the outstretched platform. To his astonishment, a beaked head appeared, and then the massive winged torso of the gryphon. The creature seemed too big to fit through the gryphon port, but then it folded its wings and stepped inside. A rider had flattened himself to the gryphon's back to duck under the doorway, but now that the beast was inside the ship he leaped lightly down from the saddle. Alexander immediately recognized him as the blond-haired boy who had swooped at him up on deck. The flyer was lightly built, and not quite as tall as Alexander. The flyer had to stand on his tiptoes as he reached up and scratched the gryphon's horse-like ears. "Good boy, Lemondrop," said the flyer, and the beast narrowed its yellow eyes to slits and purred with satisfaction. "We're off to sea at last, with no more of this infernal waiting."

For the first time, the boy noticed them standing there. "Who are you?"

"I'm the one you had a good laugh at up there on the deck!" Alexander hadn't expected himself to be so angry, and the tone of his voice surprised him. The gryphon gave him its full attention and uttered a low growl.

"Easy, Lemondrop." The boy patted the gryphon's nose fondly. Alexander found himself staring in curiosity at the boy, who, though not especially big, was almost breathtakingly handsome, with fine, classic features, almost like a Greek statue brought to life. Alexander didn't normally notice such things, but there was just something about the boy that made one stare. Part of it was also that he had very blue eyes, as intensely bright in their own way as the gryphon's. "He's very protective. Just like a big dog, really. I'm sorry, by the way, if I gave offense up there on deck. I was just having a bit of fun. You sailors have a notoriously poor sense of humor."

"Oh, please! There was nothing funny about it."

"Says you. Ha! It actually was quite funny, at least from my point of view. The other sailors seemed to find it rather humorous too. Now, I know Mr. Higson here, but I haven't seen you before. You must be one of the new ensigns."

"Alexander Hope."

"A pleasure to meet you, Mr. Hope."

"And you are?"

"Lord Parkington." With that, the flyer turned away, took the gryphon by the halter, and led him deeper into the gryphon stables.

Alexander looked at Roger, who simply shrugged and offered another of his quick grins, then led the way out of the gryphon deck. Alexander was only too happy to leave. The way those beasts looked at him with their yellow eyes made him nervous. There was something in the look that relayed the fact that they were hungry. Alexander reasoned that a gryphon was part lion, after all, and a lion didn't have many qualms about what it ate, whether it was sheep, goats ... or ensigns. He listened to the iron gate snick shut behind them with a certain amount of relief. Even the marines' quarters smelled better and seemed more inviting than the gryphon stables.

"I've never met an actual lord before," Alexander said. "He seemed a bit high and mighty."

Roger snorted. "That's just your typical flyer mentality," he said. "The way they act, you'd think each of them was flying around with the *Resolution* between his legs, instead of a single devil-beak."

Alexander smiled at that ridiculous image. "Well, I suspect Lord Parkington might be a bit more haughty than most."

"He's the earl of something or other. I can't remember. His father died young, you see, which meant the title passed to him. What matters is that he's a first cousin of the king."

Alexander felt a pang. He knew a bit about losing one's father. He wondered if perhaps Lord Parkington had a stingy uncle who had sent him off to sea, though he suspected the circumstances might be different in a lordship's case.

"Thank you for the tour," Alexander said. "This is quite a ship."

"Quite a ship? Now, that's an understatement if ever I heard one." Roger appeared a little taken aback. "We're only getting started, you know. There's so much to explain, plus I've got to get you settled in our new quarters. Come on!"

CHAPTER 3

By the time they had finished touring *Resolution*, Alexander was thoroughly exhausted and feeling more than a little overwhelmed. He had seen the sea for the first time, been rowed out to a Royal Navy ship of the line, and met both a gryphon and an earl face to face. So much in one day, and the day was far from over.

The *Resolution* had left the harbor, her sails unfurling to catch the full sea breeze. Driven by the wind, the massive ship now cut through the waves off the English Channel, sending up a salt spray that made the forward deck slippery with ice. The ship creaked and groaned like some living creature as wind fluttered the sails and whistled in the rigging. It was a contented sound, like a large dog might make when you scratched its belly. He knew *Resolution* was just a boat made of wood and iron and hemp, but the ship somehow seemed glad to be at sea again.

The day was as cold and bitter as ever, but the overall mood of the ship and crew added warmth to the winter air. Alexander still felt disoriented by the roll of the ship in the open sea, but he was getting better at keeping his balance as he followed Roger up and down ladders, and across decks.

Everywhere they went, the rest of the crew appeared to understand their duties. Men and boys were busy going about their business and running a dozen errands as if it were the most important thing they had ever done. It all seemed very mysterious to Alexander, who didn't have any duties at all.

"You there, watch where you're going!" shouted an impatient young officer, who was busy overseeing a group of sailors pulling hard at a line that stretched toward the masts high above.

Roger just laughed as they sidestepped the men, but Alexander felt his cheeks reddening again. He couldn't remember the last time he had been embarrassed this often during a single day.

"Don't worry," Roger said. "You'll feel better once you get some food into you. It's almost dinnertime! While we're at it, we may as well show you where you're going to sleep."

Roger strode confidently across the deck, dodging the busiest of the men, and Alexander did his best to follow in the ensign's wake. When Roger went below again, Alexander was right behind him. Somehow, they were in a different part of the ship altogether that Alexander hadn't seen before. H.M.S. *Resolution* just seemed to go on and on.

"Here we are," Roger finally announced, and pointed out the way with a flourish. "The ensigns' quarters."

Alexander entered a narrow, cramped room that was lit by several lanterns hanging from the low ceiling. A window at one end provided a view of *Resolution's* stern, where the white churn of the wake was just visible. Without the window, the room would have been quite claustrophobic. Several other boys wearing ensign uniforms sat around a large table, being served by a pair of rather grubby looking sailors. All eyes turned to stare at Alexander.

"Hello everyone and meet the newest member of the madhouse!" Roger announced.

"I'll have to set another place," grumbled one of the servers, moving off to rummage through several boxes and sets of shelves nearby. "Neptune knows if I can find a clean plate and cup."

"And who might you be?" asked one of the ensigns off-handedly, spearing a roll with a large knife.

"He's the one who performed such a splendid dive when that bloody gryphon swooped down," said a boy with an Irish accent. "Nice bit of athletics, that was!"

Several of the ensigns laughed. "He's not the only one who's ever done that," someone added, and Alexander felt a bit better.

"Have you got a name?" asked the ensign with the knife.

"Alexander Hope."

"Mmm. You shall be Mr. Hopeless then." The other ensign was now buttering the roll with the knife, which was much too large for the task, but he seemed to manage it well enough. "I am Ensign Fowler. Well, we do have a few rules, Mr. Hopeless. First, you should know that I am the senior officer here."

Alexander gave the other boy a closer look and saw that he was older than most of the others. He glanced over at Roger, and noticed that his tour guide was not smiling, for once.

"As such, I get a levy from the more junior officers that includes you taking one of my watch duties each month, half of your daily rum ration, clean shirts—and anything else that I decide."

Roger spoke up. "Now see here, Fowler—"

The two thuggish-looking ensigns sitting beside the older boy shifted as if preparing to get up, and Roger fell silent.

"You were saying something, Higson?"

"Oh, never mind."

"That's what I thought. Now, do take a seat, Mr. Hopeless. Our serving man here has found you a clean plate, I see, so that's something."

Alexander didn't move. He stood up straighter, bringing himself to something like attention. Fowler stared at him with a look of amusement. "Oh, we have a proper ensign for a change! It's about time, I can tell you."

"Excuse me, sir, but I don't see how outranking me gives you a right to my food or possessions."

Fowler's grin faded. "Snotty, since you're new here I'll pretend I didn't hear you question me. Just this once, mind you." He used the big knife to neatly slice an apple. "Now, I do believe I told you to sit down."

Their eyes met and locked. For just a moment, Alexander had a glimpse into the other boy's heart. There was something pale and grotesque there that hid from the light, like one of those strange weeds one sometimes finds growing under a stone. It was clear he had the other boys bullied. Alexander disliked him instantly. He could see from the look in Fowler's eyes that the feeling was mutual.

Alexander realized that he wasn't going to get anywhere with Fowler. As he moved to take his seat, a sudden lurch of the ship caused him to bump heavily against the table. A mug of grog slid off the edge of the table and spilled.

Alexander reached out to catch it, but the mug was too far away. All at once, the liquid seemed to hang suspended in mid-air.

He heard someone exclaim: "What the—"

Startled, Alexander looked up, and in the next instant the liquid splashed to the floor. It all happened so quickly that no one was sure they had really seen what they thought.

"That was odd."

"What's in this grog? Must be something tropical."

"Too bad for Hopeless here," Fowler said. "He'll be giving up his ration for a week—to me."

Alexander didn't care so much about the grog —the sailors' customary drink of water, rum and lime juice—but he didn't like the idea of being ordered about. Roger was clearly too easygoing to put up much of a fight, and the Irish boy, while outspoken, seemed to know better than to cause trouble. Conversation resumed at the table, but to Alexander's ears the talk sounded stilted and wooden. He had the impression that no one else much liked Fowler's rules, either.

As he ate the warm food and felt his belly grow full, he found himself actually growing sleepy. His head had suddenly begun to throb. It had been an eventful day, to say the least, and he had not slept well the previous night in the tavern, in strange surroundings with the darkness punctuated by the snores of other sleeping travelers.

Roger saw him nodding off, and took him by

the elbow before Alexander managed to slump into his soup. He had never felt so tired. Waves of exhaustion seemed to wash over him.

"Long day, eh? Let's get you to your hammock."

Roger wasn't the only one who had noticed Alexander's weariness. "Mr. Hopeless can take midwatch," Fowler said from the head of the table. "You'll wake him, Mr. Higson, and make certain he's aware of his duties."

"Aye, aye," Roger said. He did not look happy —maybe even a little cowed. Clearly, he was afraid of the older boy. He took a firmer grip on Alexander's arm. "Come on, then."

Roger led him to a hammock that was already strung up in the narrow space at the end of the room. Apparently the ensigns lived, ate and slept in the same cramped area. It was a step up from the sailors and the marines—who had to make do among the cannons on the drafty gun deck—but only just.

Alexander eyed the hammock with more than a bit of trepidation. It was a flimsy-looking thing, like a corner of sail or a shroud in which you might wrap a dead man, not like a proper bed at all, which in Alexander's experience had four legs and a mattress.

"It does take some getting used to," Roger said with a laugh. "The trick is not to roll right out again. Don't worry, though, because you'll get the hang of it, and then this hammock will be your new best friend—when you get to spend time in it!"

Carefully, Alexander managed to edge his way into the hammock. The fabric swayed and stretched beneath him, but it managed to hold his weight. The hammock was also surprisingly comfortable. All of a sudden, shutting his eyes seemed like the most important thing Alexander had ever done before.

"Roger, I don't know what's come over me," he whispered. "I'm so tired and my head aches."

"Dealing with Fowler has been known to do that."

"You've been very kind to me. I hope that I can be a good friend to you."

"Don't mention it, Alexander. Now get to sleep." His smile slipped a bit as he looked back over his shoulder at the table where Ensign Fowler presided. "Your watch will be here before you know it."

❈ ❈ ❈

It seemed he had hardly fallen asleep when someone was shaking him awake.

"Alexander! Wake up!"

He jolted upright and would have rolled right out of the hammock if Roger hadn't been there to steady it. He had been dreaming of home: sunshine, fields to walk upon, and of his big, soft bed. In the mixed-up way of dreams, he had somehow imagined there were tiny gryphons flitting about the empty rooms at Kingston Hall. He opened his eyes to see the dark ensigns' cabin and smelled the stale air. The dream slipped away, and he realized that this hammock was now his bed and this ship was now his home.

"What is it?" Alexander groaned.

"Time for your first duties." Roger seemed cheerful despite the hour. "You must have been having a good dream. I practically had to dump you on the deck to wake you."

"I was dreaming about gryphons."

Roger grimaced. "Well, it's a good thing I woke you, then. I'm not sure I'd trust a gryphon not to eat you in your sleep, whether you dreamed him up or not."

"That's not exactly a reassuring thought." He recalled Lord Parkington's gryphon, Lemondrop. He thought about the beast's bright, yellow eyes and shuddered. He couldn't imagine why the flyers would want to ride a beast that was better suited to a nightmare.

Alexander rolled awkwardly out of the hammock and shrugged into his stiff new sea cloak. He'd been so tired that he hadn't even undressed for bed. All around them were strung the hammocks of the other sleeping ensigns. As silently as they could, they slipped from the ensigns' quarters.

But as he made his way through the ship and up on deck, he soon discovered that the *Resolution* was never truly silent or sleeping. Because the ship sailed on through the night, a portion of the crew was required to be on duty to trim the sails and perform dozens of other duties that kept the ship running. A certain number of men also had to keep a lookout at all times for enemy ships. England's enemies never truly slept, either, and there was always a danger of encountering a Napoleonist patrol or a raiding flight of gryphons that in an instant could tear the ship's sails to shreds with their razor-sharp claws or strafe the deck with bomblets or pistol shots. Tonight, however, they were still very close to English waters and so it was doubtful that the Napoleonists would be so daring on a cold winter's night.

"You have midwatch," Roger explained as they made their way on deck. "Each watch is four hours, and midwatch is midnight to four o'clock in the morning. Those aren't anyone's favorite hours—not if you like your sleep, and who doesn't—but at least you'll be early for breakfast."

"Four hours doesn't seem too bad."

"It doesn't seem that way at first, but on a night like this the cold soaks into your bones. Plus the ensigns have classes tomorrow morning, and word is that our new teacher is a good friend of the captain and fancies himself something of a scholar, which is bad news for us. He'll actually want to teach us something, so that means more work for us."

"I reckon this was supposed to be Fowler's watch."

"As a matter of fact, it was. But as the senior ensign he is within his right to assign the watch to someone else. I suppose he wants to break you in a bit after you stood up to him at dinner. Fowler isn't one you want to cross, and his friends Lloyd and Sweeney aren't much better. Keep your head down and do what he says, Alexander, and you'll be fine."

"I thought we were here to fight the French and that usurper Napoleon, not each other."

"If I were you, I wouldn't raise that particular issue with Fowler." Roger snorted, then seemed to grow thoughtful. "You know, that was a funny thing at dinner, how that splash of grog just seemed to hang in the air. I thought it was just me, but the others saw it too."

"After the day I had, I wouldn't trust anything my eyes saw." He had forgotten all about the episode, but now that Roger mentioned it, it had been strange. "Here I am starting my second day after a few hours of sleep in a hammock, and lucky you gets to be my guide again."

"I don't mind so much. Most of the officers

are sleeping, so there's no one watching your every move and correcting you every step of the way. You'll see that during the day they all do that, trying to impress the captain with how sharp-eyed they are."

"And is he impressed?"

"Let's just say Captain Bellingham isn't easily impressed by anyone—or anything, for that matter. But a word to the wise, Alexander. The captain doesn't sleep well—I don't know that he sleeps at all—and sometimes he'll come up on deck to keep an eye on things. Like as not, he throws an old cloak over his shoulders so you can't tell it's him."

Roger explained an ensign's duties on midwatch. On a ship the size of the *Resolution*, he would not be officer of the watch—the officer in charge. That duty fell to a lieutenant or one of the more experienced ensigns. Alexander would serve as second in command. He would observe the helmsman and make certain that he followed the course on the ship's compass set by the captain. He would also be expected to walk about the deck to make certain that none of the sailors or the marines posted as sentries were sleeping. Here in the English Channel, there was always a danger of running into a Napoleonist ship or a sudden aerial attack by enemy gryphons.

"That doesn't sound like much," Alexander said, feeling a bit disappointed.

Roger clapped him on the shoulder, though Alexander barely felt it through the thick cloak. "Not to worry, but if we sight the French, you'll take command of a gun crew."

The thought made Alexander a little excited—and sick to the stomach. He really hoped that the Napoleonists would not show themselves tonight.

The officer of the watch was Lieutenant Swann, the same officer Alexander had met when he first came aboard the *Resolution*. Swann was busy working out some arrangement of the sails with several of the crews, and he only acknowledged Alexander with a hurried nod. Roger wasn't on duty, so he wished Alexander good luck and went below to try to get more sleep.

Alexander found himself without a great deal to do. The truth was that he didn't have the first idea of how to run a ship, or what was really required of an ensign. He was an officer, so he was in charge ... of what? He lingered for a while within sight of Lieutenant Swann, just in case the man should need him or have orders for Alexander. But the lieutenant and the rest of the crew seemed to have everything in hand and paid Alexander no mind. He tried to puzzle out what they were discussing, but he kept overhearing words like "mizzen" and "topsail" that may as well have been French.

He noticed that near the massive ship's wheel

was a large hourglass. Every half hour, a Royal Marine came and turned the timer just as it ran out of sand. He then gave the brass ship's bell a quick tug. Alexander had been hearing this bell continually all day, without really realizing its purpose. Now, he realized the bell was how the officers and crew measured time. The bell gave rhythm to life aboard the *Resolution*, much as the clock might in a town square or the crowing of roosters at dawn in the country.

After watching the hourglass being turned and the bell being rung several times without being called upon by Lieutenant Swann, Alexander decided to spend some time exploring the deck on his own. He was also afraid that if he stood in one place much longer, he would either fall asleep —or freeze. It was still bitterly cold.

Although there were a few men about on deck, it wasn't nearly as populated as during the day. Alexander soon found himself far toward the front of the ship, where no one else seemed to be. He hooked an arm securely through the rigging near the forward mast to keep his balance as he gazed up at the night sky.

The stars had come out, and the air was so clear and cold that the celestial points of light shimmered and sparkled. It was hard to believe that they were distant suns, perhaps with planets all their own. The thought made Alexander feel very alone as the *Resolution* slipped through the vast and empty sea. His nose was suddenly runny, and his eyes teared up. He tried to tell himself it was only on account of the cold. Alexander resisted the urge to wipe his nose with the sleeve of his coat. As he stood looking up at the sky, he became aware of voices nearby.

"Come now, give us another drink."

"You've had enough, you have. Share it, why don't you!"

The voices startled Alexander, and it took him a moment to locate the men in the darkness. He now saw that three men stood in the lee of the forward mast, seeking what shelter they could from the winter wind.

"I won this bottle fair and square, and I mean to drink it."

"Hush now! If we get caught, the captain will have us in irons."

Now Alexander was certain the men had not seen him. There was also something familiar about the voices. He chanced a look between the ropes, and in the starlight he could make out the men's faces. He recognized the three sailors who had rowed him to the *Resolution*. He gulped, hoping that they hadn't seen him. The big one had made no bones about the fact that he gladly would have thrown Alexander into the harbor, given half a chance.

He wondered what to do. He might be able to slip away before the men saw him, or stay hidden.

Maybe he should report this to Lieutenant Swann. He had half made up his mind to do just that, when he had a thought. *I am a ship's officer. Me.* If the men were doing something they should not, it was his duty to stop it, and stop it now—not go running to the lieutenant like some tattle-tale schoolboy.

Alexander took a deep breath and stepped out from behind the mast. The three men gave a start—obviously they had thought themselves alone on this section of the deck.

"What's going on here?" Alexander demanded. His voice sounded brittle and angry in the winter air—older somehow—and that gave him confidence, though his heart was pounding. These were grown men, veteran sailors, and the biggest one towered over Alexander.

"Just having a bit of fun," the big one said. He didn't seem all that worried about Alexander's arrival. In fact, Alexander couldn't be sure on account of the darkness, but something in the man's voice made him think the sailor might be smiling. "We didn't think anyone else was about."

"Well, *I* am about. And you seem to be drinking on duty."

The big one squinted at him. "You're the new ensign, ain't you? Mr. Hope. The one who looked green about the gills before we left the harbor, ha, ha! Let me tell you how it is, young sir. This is usually Mr. Fowler's watch, you see, and he don't mind—"

"I am not Mr. Fowler!" Anger boiled up in Alexander at the mention of the bullying ensign, whom he suddenly suspected was not a very good officer. "I remember your name. You're Jameson, aren't you?"

"Yes ... sir."

"And you?" Alexander looked at the other men.

"I'm Wilcox and this here's Kineke, sir."

"I want you to toss that bottle in the sea."

"You what?"

"Do it now!"

The big man didn't need to be told twice. He hurled the bottle overboard. He looked back at Alexander, clearly unhappy. "There," he said. He wasn't smiling now.

"I want to see you three working. Coil those lines there, and keep a sharp eye on the horizon. There are Napoleonist ships about, and they would like nothing better than to catch us unawares. And no more drinking on duty, or by Neptune, you'll have more than me to answer to next time."

"Yes, sir."

Alexander clasped his hands behind his back so that the sailors wouldn't see that they were shaking—and it wasn't from the cold. He waited to make certain the men got to work, and then turned to leave. As he walked away, he noticed another figure standing quietly in the shadows just a few feet away. The tall, bulky figure wore an officer's great coat, but he was bareheaded in the cold, his long dark hair tied back in a queue. Alexander hadn't seen the other officer standing there, and he was sure the sailors hadn't either, but the man had been close enough to hear everything that had just happened. The man's face was shrouded in darkness, but he gave Alexander a nod.

As he continued walking back toward the wheel, it took Alexander a moment to realize that he had just met the captain.

CHAPTER 4

The classroom aboard *Resolution* was unlike anything Alexander had expected. Mostly, his schooling at Kingston Hall had involved a series of tutors, most of them not much older than Alexander, who taught him Greek history and mathematics and Latin in exchange for room and board, plus whatever small sum his uncle had been willing to pay. Alexander almost always took his lessons in the library, surrounded by richly bound leather volumes. This was the room where his uncle retreated in the evenings to smoke his pipe and drink brandy, and the soft leather chairs were the best in the house—most of the other furniture had long since been sold off or crated up.

Alexander had been no great student, but he liked the stories of the ancient Greeks well enough. It was reading the stories in the original Greek that gave him a headache. On the dullest afternoons, sleepy after lunch, both he and the tutor sometimes nodded off over their books.

The classroom aboard *Resolution* was nothing more than a space that had been cleared on deck, never mind the biting wind or the fact that sailors were busy hauling and shouting all around them—even in the rigging overhead. The noise and cold assured that there would be no napping in this classroom. Instead of chairs, the students sat on benches or small casks, tucking their hands deep in their cloaks to stay warm. One or two swiped at their noses with their sleeves, a reminder as to why ensigns had been given the despised nickname "snotty."

At the back of this makeshift classroom, occupying a bench of their own, sat Fowler, Sweeney and Lloyd, all in a row. Fowler looking particularly well rested, and no wonder, considering that Alexander had taken his watch. His own eyes felt red and itchy from lack of sleep. Fowler saw him watching and gave Alexander a crooked, knowing smile. Alexander looked away.

In addition to the ensigns of *Resolution*, the class also contained half a dozen flyers. These boys sat all in a group off to themselves, their bright blue uniforms making a splash of color on the deck on what was an altogether gray and overcast morning. Lord Parkington was among them, and Alexander tried to catch his eye, but the boy was too busy chattering with the other flyers.

While the Royal Navy ensigns ran the gamut in size and shape, from hulking thugs like Sweeney and Lloyd to mere waifs like the Irish boy Liam Fitzgerald, the flyers were smallish and compact like gymnasts. Their size was dictated by necessity, for sometimes two or three flyers climbed aboard a single gryphon if they were making a pass to drop bomblets or aerial caltrops. In battle, there was generally a flyer who piloted the gryphon and a stern rider. Alexander was relieved that the flyers had left their gryphons chained safely below. Despite the fresh air, his nose seemed to detect a whiff of the gryphon smell—a bit like wet cat—on the flyers' uniforms, unless it was only his imagination.

And then there was the teacher. Although Alexander had seen him come aboard, he hadn't gotten a close look at him. Alexander had expected a young man, much like his previous tutors. But the man who hurried toward them across the deck, leaning into the wind, was much older—well into his thirties, at least. He was extremely tall and thin in a hungry way. There was a bump high up on his forehead that very well may have come from forgetting to duck through a hatch. He wore round, wire-rim spectacles that gave him a scholarly appearance, softening the piercing glare of his hawkish eyes as he looked around at the ensigns. He cleared his throat to get their attention, even though they were all staring at him.

"I am Professor Hobhouse," he announced, slightly out of breath. "We will begin our lesson this morning with mathematics in general and the determination of speed and distance in particular."

He grasped his hands behind his back and began to pace. As he did so, he appeared to stoop over, as if the air itself was rather heavy for his narrow shoulders. "Now, here is the situation. Two ships start from the same harbor at the same time, but they are traveling in opposite directions. One vessel moves two knots per hour slower than the faster vessel. At the end of a ten-hour period, they are twenty leagues apart. How many leagues had the slower ship traveled at the end of the ten hours?"

All the ensigns and flyers were equipped with small blackboards. There soon came the sound of chalk clicking on slate. It was a relatively simple problem, but Alexander struggled a bit with the division. How many times did six go into twenty?

Professor Hobhouse paced in front of their group. He seemed to be humming a little tune to himself, the way that impatient people sometimes do when they are put upon to wait. Alexander noticed that up close, the teacher's coat was worn to the point of being shabby, but it was clear from the cut and fabric that it had once been elegant. He could make out several places where the coat had been painstakingly patched or repaired with a few stitches. The coat seemed to have all of its buttons, but several did not match.

"Time, gentlemen! Let us see how you did, shall we?"

Some of the ensigns grumbled, and the bits of chalk made a few final clicks against the slates. One by one, the teacher took up an ensign's slate to look at the answers. Some he returned with a nod, while others received only a sigh and a shake of the head. There seemed to be more of those. Fowler, Sweeney and Lloyd all earned looks of exasperation.

"We have some work to do, I fear," Professor Hobhouse remarked to no one in particular.

When he got in front of Alexander, Professor Hobhouse grabbed up his slate and squinted at it. "Your handwriting leaves something to be desired, Mr. Hope," he said. "Though you do see to have the right answer, if I can decipher your chicken scratch. Do work to improve that, Mr. Hope. A neat hand is a sign of a gentleman, or of a Royal Navy officer."

"Yes, sir."

Hobhouse moved on to the row of flyers. Mostly, he seemed pleased with their work. He paused in front of Lord Parkington and took the flyer's slate. "Nicely done, my lord," Hobhouse said. "There does seem to be promise for some of you, at least."

Fowler muttered something, but the wind snatched the words away before Alexander could quite hear it. On either side of Fowler, Sweeney and Lloyd snickered.

Professor Hobhouse stalked over and stood in front of them. "Do you have something to say, Mr. Fowler?"

Fowler seemed to think about it for a moment, then blurted out: "We're sailors! We need to know the winds and tides, and how to aim a thirty-two pounder! I don't see the point of all this schooling." He paused. "And I don't like being ordered about by a civilian."

Alexander held his breath. He hated to admit to himself that he and Fowler agreed upon something, but he had been thinking much the same thing, though he never would have said it directly to the teacher. Hobhouse only clasped his hands firmly behind his back and walked in his stooped way back to the front of the class, where he straightened up to his full, rather impressive height and cleared his throat to speak.

"It is true that I am a civilian. But I would remind you, Mr. Fowler—and everyone else—

that on this ship I carry the courtesy rank of lieutenant. Just as does the surgeon, who is also a civilian. So you see, I do outrank you. If that does not satisfy you and you perhaps want to take up this issue with Captain Bellingham, then I would encourage you to do so." Professor Hobhouse paused as if considering that point. "I might add that the captain does not have a great deal of patience with ensigns who don't wish to study. He would surely consider this to be shirking one's duties. Now, if anyone would like to go speak to the captain now, I shall gladly dismiss you from class."

At that suggestion, no one moved, and not a single ensign would meet Professor Hobhouse's owlish glare.

He cleared his throat again.

"Now, would anyone care to tell me the answer to the following question: You are in port and wish to purchase two books and new socks. You have five pounds to spend. If you buy two books for three pounds, eight shillings how many pairs of socks can you buy for sixty pence apiece?" The teacher then went on to explain how, exactly, one might determine the answer. Alexander found it somewhat difficult to concentrate, considering that they were surrounded by the busy crew, who regarded the foundering class of ensigns with open amusement.

They struggled through another problem, this

one having to do with the trajectory of cannonballs, with more of the ensigns getting the answer right. Professor Hobhouse nodded with something approaching satisfaction, but he could see that he was losing the attention of the young officers.

"Perhaps we have gotten off to a poor start in studying mathematics first," Hobhouse announced. "Though I suppose we have many more painful hours ahead of us, judging by the dismal showing. I can only hope some of you shall make better sailors than scholars, else-wise we shall set out for Dover and end up in Madagascar, I dare say. In any case, I believe we shall change our course of study for the remainder of this class."

Alexander was fully expecting that they would now embark on something as scintillating as Latin or grammar, and he just barely managed to suppress a yawn. Beside him, Roger wasn't as successful, opening his mouth wide enough to catch swallows, let alone flies, which earned him a sharp look from Professor Hobhouse. "Do try to stay awake, Mr. Higson."

They watched the teacher go to a sea chest that had apparently been brought up earlier and placed on deck. Alexander assumed it was full of textbooks. But to his surprise, Professor Hobhouse opened the lid and took out a sword. Roger had been in the middle of another yawn, but instantly his mouth snapped shut.

"One of the skills the captain has asked me to teach you is fencing," Hobhouse announced. The teacher was a gangly man and did not appear particularly athletic, but he held the sword easily enough. He swung the blade and it made a singing sound in the winter air. "If you are called upon to board an enemy ship, you could certainly take up a cutlass and hack away at the enemy—which is what most of our sailors do—but your chances of success and survival will be substantially better if you have a few basic sword-fighting skills."

He had each of them come forward to take a sword. These were practice weapons, pitted from the salt air, with stains that may have been rust—or old blood. The gouged blades and worn grips showed that they were well used, and they did not have especially sharp edges. But the sword points were real enough, and the blades could certainly do damage.

"I've been handling a sword for years," Fowler muttered to Sweeney and Lloyd. He swung the sword impressively. He snorted. "I don't need a schoolteacher to show me how to skewer a Napoleonist."

Hobhouse gave no sign of having overheard. "Now pair off," he said. Alexander had meant to team up with Roger—whom he doubted would try to kill him right off—but in the ensuing shuffle he somehow found himself face to face with Lord Parkington. Alexander noticed that unlike some of the other ensigns, there was nothing awkward about the way the flyer held a sword. He supposed that a lord might have had some lessons with a blade.

"Too bad for you," Parkington said. "Your second day on the ship and I'm about to carve you up like a roast beef."

The flyer's blue eyes glittered in his handsome face, and Alexander wasn't sure if the other boy was smiling in amusement or in anticipation of serving Alexander up like Christmas dinner. As he faced his opponent, Alexander couldn't help but notice that his lordship's uniform was richly made and immaculately clean. It seemed unfair that one person should have so much—nobility, wealth, and good looks—and Alexander fought down the urge to slash outright at that perfect face. It was some consolation that the other boy was shorter than Alexander and thinner—though he seemed to have a great deal of confidence for a relatively small boy.

"Balance is key when fencing," Professor Hobhouse said. He struck a stance that he wished the ensigns to imitate. "If you slip or lose your footing, you've likely lost your life in an actual fight. Keep your chin up. Keep your other arm behind you. It keeps it out of harm's way and helps improve your balance. You don't want to swing your blade wildly—you're not chopping wood or swatting flies. Keep it out in front of you."

Professor Hobhouse might have said more, but he was interrupted by Lieutenant Swann, who had ambled over with some of the crew. Mathematics wasn't much of a spectator sport, but sword fighting lessons were something else altogether. "I see that you are finally teaching these young gentlemen something useful," he said. "Might I be able to assist you in the lesson?"

"By all means, Mr. Swann." Hobhouse nodded politely as the lieutenant drew his sword and struck an *en guarde* position.

The blades slithered together as the two men tested each other. Alexander saw that Lieutenant Swann could barely suppress his confident smile. Clearly, he thought he was about to look good in front of the ship's young ensigns.

Something unexpected happened next. Hobhouse struck the lieutenant's sword hard, then stepped back quickly. Lieutenant Swann rushed to fill the gap, but as he did so the teacher sprang forward to meet him, using the momentum to swirl his own blade around the lieutenant's sword, which was suddenly no longer in his hand. Professor Hobhouse caught the sword in his free hand and pointed both glittering blades at the lieutenant's chest. Astonished, Lieutenant. Swann could only stare helplessly at the sword points.

"It's all in the footwork," Hobhouse said. And in one smooth motion he reversed the captured sword and offered it back to the lieutenant with a polite bow. "Thank you so much, Lieutenant Swann. That was an excellent demonstration."

"Why, of course." The lieutenant seemed flustered as he took his sword back and sheathed it. He then hurried off, announcing as he did so: "I must return to my duties."

"Now you, boys," Professor Hobhouse said.

The clash of metal soon rang out across the deck. Lord Parkington came right at him, but Alexander beat the flyer's sword aside and lunged. His lordship managed to step back just in time to keep from getting a very nasty poke. He circled Alexander more cautiously now as their two swords clicked against each other.

Suddenly, there was a cry of pain. Alexander glanced over to see that Fowler had cut a gash across Liam's face. The Irish boy did not drop his guard, but gripped his cheek with his free hand, circling Fowler warily. Blood ran between his fingers. Fowler was smiling. Liam didn't make another sound, even though the wound must have been painful.

Hobhouse stepped between them. "Come lad, press this against it," the professor said, giving the Irish boy a clean handkerchief. "The surgeon will need to sew that up, I fear. I will take Mr.

Fitzgerald below. Mr. Higson, do run ahead and fetch the surgeon."

"Aye, aye, sir!"

"The rest of you, don't even think of touching those swords until I've returned!"

With that, Hobhouse was gone, gripping Liam's shoulder in a reassuring manner as they made their way to the surgery.

Fowler walked over and used Liam's coat to wipe clean the bloody blade. "Ugh, but this smells like rotten potatoes. I can tell an Irishman's been wearing it. It could use with a good washing!" He then speared it with the sword and started toward the ship's rail. Clearly, he intended to pitch Liam's coat into the sea. Alexander suspected that it was the only coat Liam owned.

"Stop!" he cried, and stepped in front of Fowler to block his path.

"Mr. Hopeless," Fowler said. "Just what do you think you're doing?"

"Put down that coat."

"Make me." Fowler took a step forward, and Alexander raised his sword.

"You want to fight me?" Fowler smiled. "I suppose then that you'll soon be joining your Irish friend in the surgery." With that, he threw the coat at Alexander and lunged forward.

Alexander barely managed to knock the sword aside. Fowler struck at him again and Alexander retreated. The other ensign was older and stronger, and clearly more experienced with a sword. His next thrust caught Alexander in the shoulder. The sword was dull and he dodged at the last moment, but the blade still struck him a glancing blow, ripping his coat. Fowler's face was so close that Alexander could smell his breath. It reeked of grog and onions. "You fight worse than a Frenchman," Fowler said. "I'm going to put this sword right through your lungs, snotty."

Alexander remembered how Professor Hobhouse had stepped back to throw his opponent off balance, and he mimicked that same movement now. Fowler had to overreach to bring his thrust close to Alexander, who brought his sword down on Fowler's, forcing the other ensign even further off balance. Alexander's sword was turned the wrong way to strike, so he swung his fist instead and smashed Fowler in the chin with the wide iron hilt. The other ensign went down in a heap.

"Mr. Hope! Mr. Fowler! Belay that this instant!" Lieutenant Swann shouted at them in his full command voice, clearly angry. He hurried toward them, red faced and puffed up like a storm cloud. Considering that the lieutenant was generally calm, the sight of him so clearly angry was even more frightening. He looked as if he might rip them both to pieces. "What is the meaning of this?"

Alexander wasn't about to turn tattler

regarding the fact that Fowler had been about to pitch Liam's coat into the sea, and the other ensign was too busy picking himself up off the deck and rubbing his bruised chin to reply.

"Speak up!" Lieutenant Swann's face was very red indeed. When neither boy answered, he continued to shout. "Have it your way then, by Neptune! But you'll both be serving extra watches. And perhaps a good caning will serve as well! We shall see! What utter fools you are! Is it any wonder it's against orders for ensigns to go about armed with swords!"

Lieutenant Swann berated them both for a full two minutes in front of the other ensigns and most of the crew, who had gathered around to watch. When he finally let them go—snatching away their swords first—Alexander wandered back toward the classroom area. Professor Hobhouse still had not returned from the surgery, but Roger was already back.

Roger was now staring at him, open mouthed, as if Alexander had just done something incredibly stupid or very brave—perhaps a little of both.

But it was Lord Parkington who spoke up. "Very cheeky of you, for a sailor," his lordship said, and smiled. "I thought that only flyers were that reckless."

Alexander didn't have time to answer. A marine had appeared, looking very tall and intimidating, and asked for Mr. Hope. "Captain Bellingham's orders, sir," the marine said, once Alexander had been pointed out. "He wants to see you in his cabin in ten minutes."

CHAPTER 5

It was only natural to think that being summoned to the captain's cabin was not a good turn of events. Even Roger—usually so positive—was not sure what it meant.

"The captain never has asked to see me," Roger remarked. "He usually just greets the ensigns in a group."

"So this is unusual?"

Roger seemed to think it over. "Well, it was Lieutenant Swann who got me on board the *Resolution*, and you say it was the captain who put you on the list. So you're his man, so to speak. It goes without saying that he might have his eye on you. And here you've gone and tried to kill one of the other ensigns, so that might be frowned upon."

"Roger, the only thing that's dry on this ship is your sense of humor."

They had rushed down from the deck and were back in the ensign's quarters, where Alexander was busy getting his uniform in order, brushing out the dirt spots in the wool coat and dabbing at the stains in his white canvas trousers. It was hard to believe that just two days on *Resolution* could have taken such a toll on his clothing. This was the very reason that some ensigns—those who could afford it—had two or even three uniforms, setting one aside deep in their sea chests for times just like this. His stingy uncle had insisted that his nephew needed just one uniform. "And I'm being generous with my money, boy, at that," his uncle had added. So Alexander brushed furiously at the uniform coat.

"That will do," Roger said, nodding at the coat. "Better to be a little dirty than to be a little late where the captain is concerned."

"I'm a bit nervous," Alexander admitted.

"My advice would be to say as little as possible other than 'Yes, sir' and maybe 'Very good, sir,' " Roger said. "If you stick with that, chances are you won't be left off at the next fishing boat we pass or busted down to powder monkey."

"That's not much of a plan."

"Do you think Admiral Nelson has a plan most of the time? Indeed not. He lets events follow their course. That's what makes him a hero. He is impulsive."

"Nelson has also lost an arm and an eye," Alexander pointed out. "It seems like a plan of action might have done him some good."

"Don't worry. If Captain Bellingham is unhappy with you, he'll make himself perfectly clear." Roger grinned. "Captain Bellingham can be, shall we say, very direct."

At that, Alexander finally pulled on his coat, Roger clapped him on the back, and he was on his way to the captain's cabin.

Fortunately, Alexander was so busy dodging grimy sailors and gear in an attempt to spare his uniform any further damage that he didn't have time to think before he arrived at the captain's quarters, where a marine stood guard outside the door. The marine was very tall, taller than the tip of the gleaming bayonet on the end of his musket, and he had the sort of alert eyes Alexander had noticed before in watchdogs. Alexander remembered what Roger had said about the marines being on board to protect the ship and officers in case of mutiny. The thought made him a bit uneasy. He might have hoped everyone on board *Resolution* would have been united against the enemy. But then he recalled the sailors he had confronted during his watch last night. Were they just the sort of troublemakers the marine here was on guard against?

"Mr. Hope to see the captain," Alexander said.

The marine simply stared straight ahead, so Alexander took it upon himself to knock on the captain's door. He heard a gruff voice reply, "Enter!"

Alexander stepped into the room and stood at attention, his hat tucked under his arm. He couldn't see the captain clearly at first because he was silhouetted against the great stern windows at the far end of the cabin. The cabin itself gleamed with polished wood and a fine carpet covered the floor. It reminded him a great deal of the minister's study in the parsonage back home.

He blinked, and became aware of a bulky man bending over a table, where a chart was spread out. The captain was not especially tall, of perhaps average height, but he had broad shoulders and a deep chest. He stepped away from the table and out of the window glare, and to Alexander's surprise the man looked much younger than he had expected. The dark hair pulled back into a queue did not show a single trace of gray. His face was not particularly handsome, lined with a bit of beard stubble as if he could use a shave, and his mouth seemed pulled down in a permanent scowl, but his bright blue eyes seemed to pierce Alexander, who at once felt the shabbiness of his uniform, his own skinniness—he was sure the captain could have snapped him in two, like a twig—and the fact that he was still very much a boy.

"Mr. Hope."

"Ensign Hope to see you, sir."

"Yes, I believe we've established that." Captain Bellingham scowled at him, but said nothing further. He walked around Alexander, inspecting his uniform.

He took Roger's advice and suppressed the urge to break the silence.

"An officer should take pride in his appearance."

"Yes, sir."

"Then what's the meaning of this?" The captain jabbed a finger into the slash Fowler's sword had made.

"I haven't had time to repair it, sir, and I have just the one coat."

"An officer should come to sea prepared, Mr. Hope."

"It was what my uncle could afford for me, sir."

"Your uncle?"

"Yes, sir. He is my guardian, and he is the one who outfitted me for the Royal Navy."

"I am acquainted with your uncle, of course, for he is the one who wrote asking me to take you into service." The captain continued walking as he seemed to think over this bit of news. "Forgive me for asking a personal question, Mr. Hope, but what has become of your father's estate at Kingston Hall?"

"My father's estate?" Alexander had been standing at attention, but he swiveled around now to look at the captain, who stood off to one side. "No, sir. Kingston Hall is my uncle's home, and I live—lived—there by his forbearance."

The captain strolled a bit more about the room. "I knew your father, Hope. And Kingston Hall most assuredly belonged to *him*. In fact, I visited once when you were a very small boy. Just an infant, really. I also know your uncle." Here the captain paused, as if he might say something more, but did not. "When he wrote asking me to take you into service, I of course accepted, to honor the friendship I once shared with your father."

It was news to Alexander that the family estate had been his father's, but he was more taken with another of the captain's revelations. "You knew my father, sir?"

"Yes, Mr. Hope, I most certainly did. We served together before your father left the navy to pursue other adventures. In point of fact, we served together as ensigns, many years ago."

"What was my father like?" The question popped out before Alexander could stop himself.

The captain paced a bit more. "Your father." Bellingham shook his head, and a faint smile flashed across his face. "He was an adventurer, a brave man, a good friend. I daresay you look a great deal like him at the same age."

Alexander felt a lump in is throat. "I can barely remember him, sir."

Bellingham nodded. "You were very young when he ... went away. Off to the Americas! England was not at war then, and he found navy duty too dull for his liking. Your father thought the world to be a very big place, and he wanted to see his share of it."

"He was never heard from again. It was assumed that his ship went down near South America."

"Yes, I know." Bellingham nodded. "It was sad news for us all. Tell me, Mr. Hope, I wonder what twist of fate would have put the estate into your uncle's hands? That is most peculiar. Kingston Hall was your father's inheritance, as he was the firstborn, and I understand that you are his only child."

"I always assumed it was my uncle's."

"And he has sent you to sea, just at the age when you might begin to question the situation. How convenient for him."

"I do not follow your meaning, sir."

"Well, Mr. Hope, perhaps I should not have mentioned it. There's nothing to be done for it now. We find ourselves in the English Channel, in the stormy winter season, with the Napoleonists on the prowl. When we return to land someday—victorious, pray Neptune—I shall help you find a solicitor to look into this matter of your inheritance, because it seems to me that Kingston Hall is rightfully yours, not your uncle's. But we must keep our thoughts on the war, and our wits about us, if we are to survive and do our duty."

"Yes, sir."

Alexander's head was spinning. Here was a man who had known his father! He longed to ask him more, but the captain seemed finished with him. Bellingham crossed the cabin and went to a writing desk pushed against the wall of the cabin, then returned with a glittering bracelet wrought in silver. He held it out to Alexander.

"This belonged to your father," Bellingham said. "He gave it to me for safekeeping many years ago, and I am sure he would wish you to have it now. Neptune knows why he thought it was so important. It is a wristling, which is out of fashion now, though it's very nicely made. In an earlier age when men wore armor, I suppose it would have been a sort of gauntlet intended to protect the wrist in battle."

Alexander studied the wristling. It was intricately designed, and yet it looked incredibly strong, as if it had been woven from a single strand of silver wire. The surface was covered with the tiny figures of sea creatures: porpoises, leaping fish, and seahorses, all encircling a mighty bearded figure that must be Neptune himself,

Lord of the Sea.

"Thank you, sir."

Captain Bellingham came up close to Alexander, practically nose to nose, and fixed him with those intense eyes. He took Alexander's shoulder in a powerful grip. "You have promise, Mr. Hope. I see a great deal of your father in you, but you seem to have a more temperate nature." He plucked again at the sword-sliced fabric. "Then again, I saw how you straightened out those sailors last night and heard about the sword lesson incident this morning from Mr. Swann. Perhaps there is a bit more of the tiger in you than you realize, eh, Mr. Hope?"

"I don't know, sir."

"Well, we shall find out." Bellingham stepped back. "Good to meet you at last, Mr. Hope. Serve me well, and I shall serve you well." He grinned. "You can start by promising not to kill any of my ensigns during fencing practice. Now, dismissed!"

❈ ❈ ❈

Midnight. Alexander found himself standing midwatch for the second night in a row. This time it wasn't Fowler's doing, but Lieutenant Swann's. Captain Bellingham may have viewed the incident involving the sword fighting lesson with something like amusement—along the lines of ensigns will be ensigns, after all—but that was not the case with Lieutenant Swann. And in all fairness, Alexander supposed that Swann could not witness outright combat between his junior officers without ordering some form of punishment.

And so Alexander was once again wandering the *Resolution's* deck in the wee hours of the morning. It was some consolation that Fowler was relegated to the same watch—and there was no handing it off to anyone this time. Alexander made a point of avoiding him.

The sea was oddly calm, the waves seeming to flow with an oily heaviness, and even the wind had died away, leaving the air crisp and pleasant. It was still cold as a guillotine's blade, but bearable without the wind. The only downside that Alexander could see was that the ship was making precious little headway toward whatever destination the captain had in mind.

Alexander was still too new to a life at sea to have any real duties, so once again he was assigned to keeping watch for enemy ships. It was not particularly difficult duty—or wouldn't have been if he wasn't so tired. He was glad it was so cold, or he might have fallen asleep.

Anyone with good sense would be in his bunk, sleeping, so he was more than a little surprised to see an officer in a flyer's uniform on deck. This was unusual because flyers did not share in the duties of operating the ship. He looked closer, and was pleased to discover that it was Lord Parkington. He was standing near the ship's rail, looking up at the stars. His lordship must have heard him approach, because without looking away from the sky he said, "You must be on midwatch because of the fight you had today with Fowler."

"I suppose I am," he said. "But what are you doing up here?"

The question sounded rude to Alexander's own ears as soon as he spoke it, but the flyer did not seem to notice. "Couldn't sleep. The gryphons snore and snap their jaws when they dream and it keeps me awake."

"Really?" The very thought sent shivers down Alexander's spine.

"That's supposed to be a joke, you know."

"Oh." Alexander failed to see how it was funny.

"The marines are by far noisier when they sleep than our gryphons."

"Sleep. I've almost forgotten what that's like."

They both leaned against the rail, looking down at the dark water. There was enough starlight to see the ripples caused by *Resolution's* passing. The moon was waxing, and they could see it reflected on the surface of the sea. Alexander let his arm hang down. Oddly enough, it almost felt as if he could touch the water.

"Mr. Hope—or may I call you Alexander?"

"Of course. But what should I call you? Your lordship?"

"My nickname at home was Toby. That's what the other flyers call me."

"Very well then, your lord— I mean to say, uh, Toby."

Alexander wasn't quite sure, but it seemed to him that Lord Parkington—Toby—was a bit nervous. That was surprising, because the young lord had seemed so self possessed and confident. Perhaps it was just friendship that he had trouble with. The thought made Alexander smile down at the sea. He put his fingertip over the path of a ripple made by the passing bow and watched as the ripple seemed to grow wider and deeper, as if it were running over his fingertip. He was so very sleepy. He let his hand droop so that all the fingers hung down, and the pattern in the water seemed to change, as if it were running between giant fingers. It was curious. He cupped his hand and scooped at the water like a child in a bathtub. Splashes erupted in the water beside the ship. Alexander was sure there must be porpoises swimming next to the *Resolution*.

"Where are you from, Alexander?"

"My uncle has lands near Surrey where I grew up. He decided that I needed a career, and so wrote a letter to Captain Bellingham, who knew my father. My late father."

"I see. I am sorry to hear that. I also lost my

father. He was a naval officer, and his ship went down in the Great Storm."

"Then why aren't you in the navy? You're a flyer."

"We kept gryphons at our estate. My father preferred the sea, but I learned to fly when I was little."

Alexander twirled his hand toward the ocean, watching as a kind of whirlpool sprang up. Until that moment, he had just assumed it was just coincidence that his own motions seemed to match that of the sea, but now—

"You're doing that!" Lord Parkington stepped away from him.

Alexander shook his head and lifted his hand close to his face. He had almost expected it to be wet, because it seemed that he had felt the cold water running across his hand. "I'm not doing anything," he said, but his voice was shaky. He wasn't so sure. It was all very strange.

They might have said more, but they were suddenly interrupted by a voice that made Alexander's belly turn cold with dread. "Look at this, a flyer and a sailor fraternizing! The next thing you know, dogs will be talking to cats!"

Fowler stepped out the shadows. He was flanked by Sweeney and Lloyd. Though Fowler was tall, he seemed dwarfed by the two beefy ensigns. Alexander sensed trouble, and he looked around for Lieutenant Swann, who was nowhere in sight.

"Be a good lord and run along now," Sweeney said to Lord Parkington. "I'm sure the gryphon stalls need mucking out. Our business is with snotty here."

Lord Parkington took a step toward the three older ensigns. Alexander realized just how small and slight Parkington was in comparison. At the same time, he could sense from Parkington's demeanor that he was completely and totally unafraid. All at once, he felt braver himself.

"You forget yourselves," Parkington said coldly. "You forget your place."

"Ha!" Fowler half barked. "We were just going to toss Mr. Hopeless here in the sea and be done with him, but maybe we shall throw you in as well, though I fear it will be harder to explain how two ensigns managed to lose their footing."

"Snotty here fell in and Lord Parkington jumped to save him," Sweeney said. "Pity about that."

Fowler smiled unpleasantly. "That's a very good solution."

Something suddenly gleamed in Lord Parkington's hand. Alexander's breath caught in his throat when he realized it was a pistol.

"One shot," Fowler said. "And there are three of us, if your lordship can't manage the math."

"Quite right," Parkington said, and cocked the pistol. It was a small and elegant weapon, but the metallic click of the hammer being cocked was very loud in the cold air. "But I only plan on shooting you."

Sweeney and Lloyd shuffled back a bit from Fowler, who seemed frozen in place. He smirked. "Would you really shoot me in cold blood?"

"It is the only blood I have. And after I have killed you, I will see to it that these other two hang—or perhaps I shall have them drawn and quartered. By the king's order, it is death for a commoner to threaten a peer."

Alexander gulped. There was such an utter coldness in the other boy that it made him afraid, even though he wasn't the one in the pistol sights.

"Our feud is with snotty." Now Fowler almost sounded like he was whining.

"Why, because he stands up to the likes of you, Fowler? I saw what happened on the deck today. Consider him under my protection. If he comes to any harm, you shall answer for it."

Fowler muttered something unintelligible, but he took a step back, and then another, before he melted away into the darkness with Lloyd and Sweeney. The pistol never wavered in the other boy's hand until they were gone.

"You could have shot Fowler and those other two bullocks still would have thrown us into the sea."

"Oh, I don't think so." Parkington gave a low

whistle, and the darkness seemed to shift behind them. Alexander became aware of a pair of yellow eyes glowing in the starlight, and beyond that, the massive hulk of a gryphon.

"You mean he's been there the whole time?"

"If any of them had taken another step, Lemondrop here would have eaten all three for a midnight snack."

"Thank you," Alexander said. "I think they really did mean to throw me overboard." He paused. "Would you really have shot him?"

"I come from a long line of ruthless people," Parkington said. "As the tenth Earl of Parkington, I like to uphold family tradition."

"I am in your debt, my lord."

"If you feel that way, Mr. Hope, then someday I shall ask you to repay it."

CHAPTER 6

The next few days passed in something of a blur as Alexander tried to fit into the busy rhythm of life aboard the *Resolution*. Bells rang, hourglasses turned, sails went up and down and up again, hurried meals were eaten, school lessons were endured, and it all seemed punctuated by a few precious hours of sleep. He felt as if everyone else was in on some secret that he didn't understand. It didn't help that the crew lived in constant fear of a Napoleonist attack, leaving them edgy and impatient with a newbie.

One good change that had come about since the confrontation on the deck with Fowler was that the bullying ensign and his cronies now left him alone. Fowler still cast a threatening glance or two in Alexander's direction—a sort of you'll get yours someday—but he kept well clear of Alexander. Lord Parkington had been extremely convincing. And Fowler wasn't so much of a fool not to understand that while Parkington was only a boy, he came from a rich and well-connected family. One word in the right ear, and Fowler might find himself serving out the rest of his naval career on a garbage scow.

Alexander had not seen much of the flyer since that night. The ship remained in reach of the shore-based French gryphon squadrons and the captain was always on alert for a surprise aerial attack, so that he kept the flyers aloft day and night on almost constant patrol.

Even with Fowler reined in, it was hardly all cozy and friendly in the ensigns' mess.

His swinging hammock was now his favorite place of all on the ship. Whenever he crawled into it, he promptly fell into a dreamless sleep, which was a welcome relief. If he had any thought at all, it was how much he missed home. At such times, in the darkness in the vast belly of the ship, he felt utterly alone. Most of the other boys had been at sea for years already, and it was hard to strike up a conversation with them, let alone a friendship. They considered Alexander a newcomer and therefore a boy who must still prove himself. Even the Irish boy, whose coat Alexander had saved during fencing class, had been standoffish—almost as if he feared that Alexander would expect friendship in return.

It didn't help that Fowler had made an enemy of him; instead of siding with Alexander, the other ensigns seemed afraid that Fowler might target them next. So far, Roger was the only real friend Alexander had made aboard *Resolution*.

It was also Roger who clarified something about Fowler that Alexander had already suspected. They were both in their hammocks, side by side, talking quietly. "You see, it's like this. Fowler is getting a bit too old to be an ensign. He's like a piece of fruit that's overripe, or better yet, milk that's gone sour!" Roger laughed so hard at his own comparison that he nearly tumbled out of the hammock. "By all rights, he should have made lieutenant by now. That's the natural order of things. But he's taken the examination once and failed. It can't help when he sees fresh new faces like yours. That's just more competition for the likes of him. Fowler's only real hope is that Captain Bellingham might make him an acting lieutenant, but that generally only happens after there's been a battle."

"Why is that?"

"It's usually because one of the officers has been killed."

That seemed like a terrible path toward promotion, but Alexander decided it was just another aspect of navy life that he hadn't yet come to understand.

Thinking about battles, he finally drifted off to sleep.

❊　❊　❊

The confrontation with Fowler overshadowed something else that had happened that same night. It had to do with how Alexander had seemed to manipulate the sea while he and Lord Parkington were talking. Alexander might have thought he had imagined it, but Parkington had noticed it too. The other boy had been taken back, even afraid, which seemed out of character for the flyer.

By the light of day, it seemed impossible that Alexander had made the cold ocean water do anything. The sea had a power and a will all its own that was beyond any human influence—with the exception of a sea elemental. And the last time there had been one of those was two hundred years ago.

Of course, the great sea elemental Sir Algernon Hope had been Alexander's great-great something or other. Where did that leave Alexander? *Feeling like a fool,* he thought, standing at the ship's rail a couple of days later as he worked up the nerve to attempt it again. This time it was daylight, and Alexander was alone. He made sure that no one was paying attention, then reached out his hand toward the sea. Nothing happened. He wasn't sure what he even *wanted* to happen. He closed his eyes tight and tried again. When he finally opened them, he saw that the sea was unchanged.

No ripples. No whirlpools. No splashes. Just the vast empty ocean. He felt a bit relieved, but also disappointed. He also felt silly. What did he think he was playing at? He was being childish, like a little boy, dreaming that he could control the sea.

He studied the waves for a while. The day was dark and overcast, with a brisk, cold wind blowing that filled the sails and moved the ship easily through the waves. Hardly a pleasant day to be standing at the rail for any length of time. He was about to turn away and find a warmer place more sheltered from the wind when he thought he might give it one more try. He reached out one hand toward the waves and willed two of the them to join together. Nothing.

"You there, Mr. Hope!" It was Lieutenant Swann, who seemed to have eyes in the back of his head for wayward ensigns. Since the incident with the fencing lesson, he had also kept those eyes carefully upon Alexander more than the others. "This is no time for dawdling, young Mr. Hope! Go join the sailing master at the forecastle, and perhaps you shall learn something yet."

Only later, when his watch had ended, and he had, indeed, learned from the sailing master—Mr. Drury—the difference between the mizzen staysail and foretopsail, did he think more about what had happened that night with Lord Parkington looking on. Surely the two of them hadn't imagined that Alexander manipulated the sea. Something *had* happened that night, even if he hadn't been able to repeat it today. There was always someone about who could do little tricks with water or fire. Maybe enough of old Algernon Hope's blood had filtered down to him for that much, at least. Perhaps he had just been going about it the wrong way.

And so he sought out the most knowledgeable person he knew aboard the ship, save for Captain Bellingham, whom he most certainly could not approach on the subject. The captain had more important things to worry about.

He found Professor Hobhouse in his cramped cabin, reading by the dim light of a candle lantern. Several books were spread on the little table, sitting beside a mug of coffee. Professor Hobhouse, like the ship's officers, had his own cabin, though it was so small there was only room for the table, a single chair, a large sea chest whose open lid showed it to be overflowing with books, and a hammock. The cabin did have a tiny porthole that let in a pale winter light that was open to the sea air, but it still smelled damp and salty in the cabin, with an underlying odor of musty books. Alexander took it all in as he stood at attention in the cabin doorway.

"Mr. Hope," Hobhouse said, peering at Alexander over the rim of his glasses. "Did you have a question about mathematical proportions?"

"No, sir."

"Fencing tactics, perhaps?" Hobhouse took a sip of the coffee, Alexander suspected, only in order to hide a smile. Hobhouse wore a pair of gloves with the fingertips clipped out, making it easier for him to turn pages and take notes while still keeping his hands warm.

"Not that either, sir."

"Oh? Well, are you planning to enlighten me, or shall I read your mind?"

"I'm here to ask you about elementals."

Hobhouse sat up straight in his chair and put down his coffee. "What an interesting subject. Those who control the elements with nothing more than their minds. These men and women have been some of England's greatest heroes, and her worst enemies. I must ask you, Mr. Hope, what could possibly be so important about elementals at the moment?"

Alexander considered how to answer that, and then evaded the question with another. "Have you ever met one?"

83

"You had better sit down, Mr. Hope. You are making me nervous standing there. Here, close the lid on that chest and have a seat. There's a good lad."

Alexander did as he was told, though the space was so tight he could barely get his knees between the chest and table. He had thought Professor Hobhouse might be annoyed with him for having interrupted his reading, but he noticed that as the ship's schoolmaster closed the book he did so with something that bordered on relief. Alexander hadn't thought about it, but aside from teaching the ensigns, Professor Hobhouse had no other real duties aboard *Resolution*. It seemed an odd life for a civilian to choose, teaching young gentlemen at sea, but it was certainly no easier eking out a living on land as a teacher. Some lucky few scholars received posts at a university, but many who loved books and learning had to scrabble for a living as best they could. It was also common knowledge that the schoolmaster was a good friend of the captain's, and that the two of them had made many voyages together.

"Don't you ever get bored down here, sir?"

"A boring day at sea is a good one. It means you are not riding out a gale, fighting the French, or making some desperate repair to keep the ship from sinking or foundering on the rocks. It's been my experience that boring days are few and far between. Ha, ha! Indeed. But I thought you were interested in elementals."

"And so I am, sir, so I am."

"It's curious that you wish to speak of it now." Professor Hobhouse gave him a knowing look—the schoolteacher had a way of making his pupils aware that he was one step ahead of them. "Has something happened, Mr. Hope?"

"Not at all, sir. I was just wondering."

Hobhouse gave him a sideways glance, as if he didn't quite believe Alexander. After a long pause he said, "Very well. Elementals are a rarity, Mr. Hope, and always have been. The power seems to be passed down through families—though there are exceptions, or maybe latent power that's lurking somewhere from some distant branch of the family tree. That's mostly the explanation for parlor and circus elementals—the ones who can do amusing tricks with a candle flame or a water glass. You have an ancestor who was an elemental, of course."

Alexander knew the stories about his famous ancestor. It was usually Sir Francis Drake who got most of the credit for defeating the armada intent on invading and conquering England. That was not the whole of the story. It was Alexander's ancestor, Sir Algernon, who had summoned the storm that wrecked the armada on the Irish coast. It was the final blow to the King of Spain's hopes of adding England to his crown.

"A distant ancestor," Alexander said.

"Actually, you are a direct descendant." Professor Hobhouse raised his eyebrows at Alexander's surprised expression. "Oh, I thought you would have known that."

"My uncle never wanted to talk about it."

"I'm sure he had his reasons. For the most part, elementals are concentrated in your great noble families—in the past, it was their ability to manipulate the elements that brought them power and wealth." Professor Hobhouse lowered his voice. "That is why, from time to time over the centuries, the king or queen became jealous and purged the great elemental families. When Oliver Cromwell came to power, he hunted them down as witches. The lords of earth, sky, fire and water have never had an easy time of it. That is one reason elementals are so few today." Hobhouse paused. "You might say we killed most of them off. And here we are without so much as a single sea elemental in our greatest hour of need, when England struggles for its very survival."

Hobhouse did not have to explain that those with the power could control just one element. That was common knowledge. "Are all elementals from noble families?"

"Not at all, Mr. Hope. Not at all. You and I both know that Napoleon Bonaparte is himself a fire elemental—an utterly terrifying thought—

and he has somewhat humble origins. No one really knows where such power originates." Hobhouse took off his eyeglasses and polished them, as if to be sure he didn't have to look Alexander in the eye as he added, "Though some say the power originates in the old Roman gods."

"We have a fire elemental. A fire lord, I should say. Everyone knows that."

"Yes, we do. Lord Wellington, Neptune be praised. England has rarely had a greater hero. He holds Bonaparte in check and keeps him from unleashing his full power, for fear of what Wellington might do in return. But at least one of Bonaparte's marshals is a sky elemental, Marshal Michel Ney. He can rip our gryphons from the air with a wave of his hand. So it would seem the Napoleonists already have us outnumbered, two to our one. The Russians have a sky elemental and three earth elementals—though one is a count with a fondness for vodka. They say he wrecked one of the Czar's own fortresses during a drunken fit in which he caused an earthquake."

Alexander asked the next question as nonchalantly as he could. "What of a water elemental?"

"You speak of a sea lord, Mr. Hope. There has not been a sea lord in an age. Not since the threat of the Spanish Armada."

"That was two hundred years ago," he remarked, half to himself.

"Perhaps we are lucky in that our enemy also lacks a water elemental. Can you imagine what it would mean to our navy if there was such an enemy?"

Alexander thought of the *Resolution*, its many guns and sailors, plus the flight of gryphons. Taken together, it was an awesome force. "One water elemental could not stop the navy."

"No, but he could turn the tide of a single battle and perhaps even of the entire war by giving the Napoleonists an advantage."

"If a person were an elemental, how would they know? How might they increase their powers?" Alexander blurted out the rest of what was on his mind before he could stop himself. He could see from his teacher's raised eyebrows that he had said too much.

"One is either an elemental, or one is not. It is not something that one can practice or develop, like skill at tying knots. Is there something you wish to tell me, Mr. Hope?" Hobhouse stared at him intently.

"No, sir."

Hobhouse went back to regarding his coffee cup. "I tried it, you know, when I was a boy. Ha, I suppose every boy has. Stared at a candle flame and willed it to burn brighter." He smiled. "Or tried to get up a gust of wind. I should think that if you were an elemental, you could make the liquid in this cup form a perfect whirlpool."

Alexander sensed that it was a trap somehow. "That's impossible, sir. You yourself said there hasn't been a sea lord in an age. Why should we have one now?"

"Perhaps it is time for a new age to begin, Mr. Hope. The war against our enemies is desperate. All the world sometimes seems arrayed against us. If you come across a water elemental, I do hope you'll tell me." He paused again. "It would be a great burden for someone to bear alone."

At that, Hobhouse reopened his book, and Alexander went to find his hammock. In the few minutes it took him to drift off to sleep, he wondered if he had made a mistake saying anything at all to the teacher. England might welcome a hero, but there had been a warning couched in what Hobhouse had said. An elemental might have a gift that made him powerful as an ancient Roman god, but it was a power that made him many enemies. Alexander felt better after talking with the professor. It seemed highly unlikely that he was any sort of elemental—at least, not a real one. That was a relief in a way—so much power would be a terrible burden as much as a gift. Even if he had such power, he would be reluctant to use it.

CHAPTER 7

Alexander woke the next morning to find that his hammock was pitching and rolling. He thought that maybe he was having a bad dream, but even after he opened his eyes wide, he could see the beams of the *Resolution* swinging wildly above him.

"All hands on deck!" someone shouted. "All hands on deck to shorten sail!"

Alexander rolled out of his hammock and promptly fell on the steeply pitched deck. The *Resolution* seemed to be tilted at an impossible angle.

"Ow." He rubbed his head where he had banged it against a post, then cried out, "What's going on?"

"It's a gale!" answered Liam, who turned out to be the one who had done the shouting. "It's come out of nowhere and caught us sideways, and if we don't reduce sail we'll be going over!"

Like most of the other ensigns, Alexander had taken to sleeping in his clothes—not only to stay warm but because it was hard to pull on clothes when one was rushing to his duty on the watch. No one wanted to waste time getting dressed when every minute of sleep was so valuable. The downside was that his clothes never really dried out but stayed damp and salty—he hated to think how he must smell. Fortunately, everyone else smelled too. He tugged on his shoes and coat, then rushed up to the deck.

The gray dawn that greeted him was wild and windy. He had almost begun to think that all the stories about storms at sea were legends or exaggerations, but the sight that greeted him now changed his mind. The sky toward France was slate gray and the clouds hung so low they nearly touched the pennants snapping in the gale. Yet it was the sea itself that took Alexander's breath away and caused his heart to hammer within his chest.

The ship rose up the side of the wave, then dropped into a trough, so that the sea seemed almost even with the ship's rail. The very tops of the waves were churned by the wind into a white, blowing froth.

"Great Neptune!" he cried.

"Aye, young sir," agreed a sailor who overhead him. "And it's Neptune we'll all be goin' to meet if we don't get them sails down."

A wave broke over the deck, flooding everyone and everything with foaming saltwater. He grabbed at a hatch cover to keep from being swept away. He saw that every third or fourth wave crashed into *Resolution*, threatening to wash men and gear over the side. Many of the men were roped together and when one was washed down, then others were able to pull him back to his feet.

"Tie on, lad!" the sailing master shouted above the roar of the wind, and shoved a rope at Alexander. He quickly looped it around his waist and tied if off with a bowline—the new knot he had been taught. It was designed never to slip loose or tighten, but to hold a loop fast.

As he took in the sights around him, Alexander reflected that Professor Hobhouse had been correct when he stated that a dull day at sea was a good one. Soon, Alexander was wishing for a dull day again.

The English Channel was notoriously stormy in winter. The waves did help to create a barrier between England and her mortal enemy, but the storms made it devilishly hard on the Royal Navy ships and crews who found themselves at the mercy of the weather.

Resolution was caught in a gale that had blown up surprisingly fast. Even a land-lubber like Alexander could see the problem, aside from the rough sea: the wind was coming at the ship sideways, catching the sails and forcing the ship too far over. *Resolution* was riding out the storm, but if the waves grew heavier or the wind howled yet harder, the ship might lean so far into the sea that she swamped. There was an additional danger that the force of the wind might carry away a mast, leaving *Resolution* doomed and helpless on the heavy sea.

"Hands aloft to shorten sail!" called a booming voice, which Alexander recognized at once as Captain Bellingham's.

Alexander looked up and saw that the captain had one arm hooked around a mast to keep from being swept away. He saw a wave crash into the captain, leaving him soaked as a wet cat. Bellingham didn't seem to notice. He pointed to some men trying to tie down a loose cannon. "Belay that and get aloft!"

Roger and Liam rushed past Alexander and swarmed up the rigging to join the hands who were already struggling with the sails overhead. Alexander moved to join them, but had to untie the safety line first. He was just starting to climb when a large figure elbowed past him, nearly causing him to lose his grip. It was Jameson, the big sailor Alexander had reprimanded for drinking on watch. He wondered if the man had nearly stepped on his hands on purpose.

It was not his first time aloft, but no matter how often he climbed the rigging, he was not sure he would ever get used to it. He had heard some sailors say they never did. Fortunately, he was not afraid of heights, though he didn't care to push his luck. One lesson Alexander had quickly learned was never to look down. That might cause you to freeze—or possibly even to fall. In a way, the gale was a good distraction. Alexander was so busy trying to climb as the ship rocked wildly, all the while being lashed by wind and salt spray, that he didn't even bother to look below.

The challenge was in climbing out over the yard to hoist the sail. The mast was vertical and the yard was the horizontal wooden crossbar from which the sails were hung. Several men had to shimmy out onto the yard, high above the deck and the churning sea. In calm weather, some men made a game of it and stepped lightly across this wooden version of a high wire. But in this gale, the men moved slowly and deliberately. One slip and it was all over—falling to the deck far below would leave a man crushed and broken, while the chances of rescue were slim if a man plunged into the roiling sea. It took many hands to pull up a wet sail—in a driving wind no less— and secure it to the yard. It was the job of the ensigns to direct the men's work. Alexander wasn't sure how he could tell these hands to do a job that they had done many times before and knew better than he did.

He followed Roger's example and worked his way out onto the yard, then shouted encouragement to the men as he tugged and pulled at his own section of sail. The wind grew even more powerful, seeming to whip Alexander's words away as soon as they left his mouth. The gale howled through the rigging and tugged at Alexander's very fingers as if trying to work them loose. It didn't help that at this height the masts carried them in a wide arc. At one point, the masts swung so far over that the yardarm—the outermost tip of the yard—very nearly dipped into one of the mountainous waves marching toward *Resolution*.

It was madness. Alexander clung to the handholds for dear life, watching in amazement as the sailors continued to work as best they could.

Then the wind shifted, snapping at them like a whip. The sudden change in direction threw several sailors off balance and they lunged desperately for handholds and footholds.

There was a terrified cry, and Alexander saw the big sailor Jameson begin to fall. The man's eyes grew wide in amazement as he snatched desperately at empty air. For a fraction of a second, it almost seemed that the wild pinwheeling of his arms would keep him in place like some ungainly bird. But then he began to go over backwards. At the last instant, Roger tried to catch the sailor and grabbed hold of his hand. But the man weighed too much, and Alexander watched in horror as the other ensign was yanked into thin air.

"Roger!" he cried. He lunged for his friend, but he was too far away.

Warning shouts went up all around him as the two fell. Their tumbling bodies just missed being broken on the deck. They plunged into the stormy sea like giant stones.

"Men overboard to larboard!" someone cried out to Alexander's left, but he doubted that anyone on deck could hear. The sailors in the rigging were helpless to do anything—the sail was finally all brought in, but one wrong step in this wind could send someone else plummeting into the sea.

Below, he saw several sailors rush to the rail. One threw a line, but the man was throwing against the wind, and the line fell well short of the two figures flailing in the water, obviously swimming for their lives. No matter how hard they swam, the ship seemed to be increasing its distance from them due to the wind and the current. Soon, the men were being swept up the side of a massive wave, being carried yet farther away.

Alexander had never felt so hopeless and useless. Here he was, high above the sea, watching two shipmates being swept away to their certain deaths. He did not know the sailor very well, but Roger was a good friend—the only one he had really made aboard *Resolution*.

Hot tears stung his eyes and burned his cold cheeks. A moment ago he had been terrified, trying to keep his balance in the rigging. Now he just felt angry. Angry at the gale, this ship, the miserable way he had been cast into this new life as an ensign. Angry that he was watching his friend drown.

He didn't think through what he did next. He simply did it. The mast swung down again and one of the huge waves loomed. Alexander dove from the rigging and rocketed into the sea. Just before he hit the water, he could have sworn he heard someone on deck shout, "The damn fool has jumped in!"

The cold of the winter sea was so shocking that it nearly stopped his heart. In a panic, he fought his way to the surface. He glimpsed the slick black sides of the *Resolution* looming above. The wind and waves pummeled him.

It was easier swimming underwater, so he held his breath and swam with powerful strokes in the direction where he had last seen Roger and the sailor. Though Alexander had never seen the sea before arriving at Spithead Harbor, he always had enjoyed swimming in the local ponds and streams around his uncle's estate. Those still pond waters were nothing like this. For one thing, they were much warmer than the wintry English Channel.

He finally came up for air, emerging from the silent world underwater to the howling of the wind and spray whipping so hard against his face that he could scarcely catch his breath. He spotted Roger and Jameson nearby and swam toward them.

"Alexander!" Roger cried. "What have you done? Now you'll drown too! The *Resolution* can't reach us. The wind and tide are against her."

He could see that Roger was sputtering seawater and struggling to stay afloat. He looked exhausted and afraid. It didn't help that he was trying to keep the sailor from going under. Big as the man was, he couldn't swim very well, but kept slapping ineffectively at the waves. Roger let go of him momentarily and Jameson went under.

"I've lost him!"

"I'll get him!"

Alexander took a deep breath and dove. His wet wool clothes were like lead weights and he kicked harder as the heaviness dragged him down. The sailor was just underwater, struggling feebly. Alexander got under him and pushed upward, helping the man toward the surface. A second later Alexander surfaced beside him. The *Resolution* seemed to have moved even farther away.

"We're doomed," Roger said. "There's no way we'll ever get back to the ship. We can't swim against this wind and this current."

Alexander knew that Roger was right. They would die here on the open sea.

That thought nearly overwhelmed him with its unfairness. But he did not feel afraid or regret jumping in after Roger. He felt himself growing angry at the waves.

Something seemed to clench inside him, the way a muscle does when you lift something extraordinarily heavy. Only this flexing wasn't in his arms or his legs or his torso, but in Alexander's mind. He felt something flow through him, something he had never felt before and couldn't even begin to describe. It wasn't an emotion like anger or fear, or a sensation like hot or cold or pain. He had felt this before in a much milder way that night when Lord Parkington had caught him absently playing with the ripples on the calm sea. Something primitive in Alexander's brain—back in the uncivilized corners where we understood the value of fire or a good, sharp stick — recognized the force flowing through Alexander for what it was. This was power. He held the feeling in his mind, keeping it there like one might cup a flame from the wind.

"Both of you grab hold of me and hold tight!"

"You can't keep us both afloat," Roger

protested. He sounded even more tired than before and his strokes had grown more sluggish.

"Just do as I say!"

Roger and the sailor took hold of his shoulders. It became considerably harder to swim, but Alexander ignored that. He focused on whatever force it was now roaring through his very veins. Instinctively, he knew what to do, even though he had never done this before.

He concentrated on the water all around him —grew angry at it like a dog that wouldn't obey— and summoned a wave. He could feel it wrapping around them.

"What's happening?" Roger cried out, clearly terrified.

Alexander did not break his concentration to reply, but reached out with his mind into the sea around them. The wave rose, growing higher and higher, then began to roll toward *Resolution*. Instead of the three of them bobbing up one side of the wave and down the other, the wave seemed to have caught them in its grip, like a fist closing around them.

The wave built speed even against the wind and rolled toward the ship. Someone on deck shouted and pointed, then another man, and another. Their cries became tinged with awe and terror as the wave towered over the *Resolution*. In another moment, it would crush the ship.

Alexander willed the water to disperse. At the

last possible instant, when the wave would have broken against *Resolution* and swamped it, the water instead subsided. One last burst of energy propelled Alexander and the two others forward, hurling them onto the deck, where they landed in a wet heap.

"Help those men!" Captain Bellingham shouted.

On his hands and knees on the deck, Alexander felt cold and exhausted. The full realization of what he had just done—leapt into a stormy ocean and bent the sea to his will— washed over him like another wave. He felt hands reaching for him, and felt a heavy blanket being draped around his shoulders. He tried to stand up, tried to tell them he was all right, but his knees buckled beneath him and Alexander fell down into darkness.

CHAPTER 8

Alexander woke up with a splitting headache. When he looked at the low ceiling, it seemed to swim in front of his eyes, and for a moment he feared that he was still under water. Then he realized he wasn't in his own hammock at all, but in the ship's surgery. He was confused, though it all came back to him in a rush—the storm, the wave, being washed up on deck. The memory of it made his head ache more sharply.

"You do seem to have a knack for getting into trouble, Mr. Hope."

Alexander turned toward the sound of the voice and saw Professor Hobhouse sitting in a chair with a book. He was looking at Alexander over his spectacles. Almost at the same time,

Alexander noticed that something wasn't quite right. He realized that the ship had stopped pitching and rolling with the storm. Bright sun streamed through the portals that illuminated the ship's surgery.

"Is the storm over?" he asked. "How long have I been here?"

Professor Hobhouse closed his book. "Three days."

"Three days!" Alexander struggled to sit up, but the room suddenly spun out of control. He groaned and let the hammock swallow him again.

"Don't let the surgeon hear you doing that or he'll want to bleed you. Relieving the miasmas of the blood, I believe he calls it. He's rather eager to use that lancet at every opportunity, but I'm afraid I threatened to use it on him in a rather nasty way if he came near you."

"I can't believe I've been sleeping here for three days. Why didn't someone wake me? I imagine the captain will be disappointed that I've been absent from duty."

"You are a curious boy, Mr. Hope. Considering that you saved the lives of an ensign and an able seaman, I don't believe the captain will begrudge you a few days to recuperate."

"What happened?"

"I was going to ask you the same thing." Hobhouse paused. "But a word of caution, Alexander. It may be wise to say little of what happened, or feign ignorance. That may be for the best until you really understand your actions. There are many forces at play here, and the less said, the better."

Alexander was a little taken aback that the schoolmaster had called him by his first name. It was one of the rare times that had happened on the ship—other than with Roger, who really didn't count. Alexander also couldn't help but notice that the schoolmaster's voice had taken on an ominous tone of warning. He wanted to ask him what he meant, but at that moment the surgeon walked in.

"Ah!" he said. "I see you're awake, Mr. Hope. Feeling better?"

"Yes, thank you, sir. I do have a terrible headache."

"You probably hit your head when you leapt from the rigging, or when you landed on deck," the surgeon said. "Perfectly normal."

Alexander would have liked to ask the doctor just what was perfectly normal about anything that had happened during the storm. But he noticed the schoolmaster give him a barely perceptible shake of the head. "Yes, I suppose you're right."

The surgeon studied him with professional interest. "You do look a bit pale." He tugged at his chin. "Perhaps I should bleed you—"

"Come now, that won't be necessary,"

Professor Hobhouse said in his stern schoolmaster's voice. It had the effect of stopping the surgeon in his tracks as he reached for a razor-sharp lancet.

Any debate over the need for bleeding was halted by the arrival of Roger, who came barreling through the door like a puppy, full of his usual energy. "You're awake!" His smile was so genuine that Alexander felt a rush of warmth toward the ensign. It didn't lessen much even when Roger grabbed Alexander's shoulder and shook him, causing his head to ache all over again. "It's good to have you back, and I'll bet your hungry. Good thing, because the captain is hosting dinner in his cabin tonight, and you're invited."

All at once, Alexander did feel starved. His stomach rumbled as if he had a cannonball rolling around in what felt like an empty, cavernous space. "That sounds perfect."

❈ ❈ ❈

Alexander might have skipped dinner altogether, as overwhelmed as he was by the conversation he'd had with Professor Hobhouse. The professor was full of cautions and warnings. But as the sun began to set over the wintry sea he realized that he was ravenously hungry. The captain's table seemed like the best place to get a decent meal.

Most of the time, the ensigns took their meals together, all seated around the same table. The food was plain—ship's biscuit, salted beef and boiled potatoes—and not especially plentiful, cooked up rather indifferently by a sailor named Stagg. He was an old sailor who would have been lost on land, but he was far too ancient for regular duty, so Stagg had been made to cook for the ensigns' mess. The captain had taken pity on Stagg, but he did not take pity in turn on the ensigns or their victuals. Stagg could boil water, make tea, and take the raw out of meat, but he was not a real cook or chef in any sense of the word.

The older ship's officers—including the surgeon and schoolmaster—ate in the gunroom. (So named for the guns that stood ready just beyond the dining table). The captain ate best of all because he received the choicest provisions, employed the most capable cook, and had money enough to set a table that fairly groaned—plus there was wine or cider instead of grog, a marked improvement. All of which made being invited to the Great Cabin to dine with the captain a very welcome event.

A short time before dinner, Alexander left the sick bay and went below to put his uniform in some kind of order. After just a short time at sea it was battered and stained, not to mention stiff with salt from being dunked in the channel. The coat hung a bit loosely on him—the meals on board were hardly filling him out.

Roger had been invited to dinner as well and was busy rummaging in his own trunk for a clean shirt. He looked Alexander up and down as he came in.

"You're a sight." He tossed Alexander a blindingly white, folded shirt. He grinned. "I suppose the least I owe you is a clean shirt. You did save my life, after all."

Alexander grinned back. He had never had a brother or anyone to wander the woods and fields with him. The estate where he had grown up was a lonely place, with no one to talk to but the servants and the itinerate tutors. He realized that Roger was his first real friend. "Thanks, Roger."

He stripped off his shirt and washed up in a basin of water that sloshed with the ship's motion, then slipped on the fresh shirt. He pulled back his hair into a tight queue. He snapped the coat a couple of times to get the stiffness out of it, then put it on. It was the cleanest he had felt in weeks.

"Ready?" Roger asked.

On the ladder they passed old Stagg, struggling with a pot of salt beef for the other ensigns' dinner. "You two, try not to fall into the sea on your way," he grumped, and then laughed so hard he nearly dropped the pot.

❀ ❀ ❀

Alexander and Roger seemed to be the last to arrive, which earned them a quick, disapproving look from the professor, but Captain Bellingham didn't seem to notice. He was deep in conversation with the sailing master, Mr. Drury, about the dangers of hoisting full sail in rough weather. The captain's Great Room was much larger than any other quarters on the ship, big enough that some of the guests had chosen to stand or walk about. The captain's room was also the only quarters on board with a row of glass windows, and light from the fading day filled the room, although the watery winter light had to be supplemented by several candles. Without doubt, it was the most elegant room on the ship, and Alexander immediately felt that he had to be on his best behavior, a feeling not unlike stepping into a church.

But it was still something of a tight fit, and most of the guests had already seated themselves around the large table, complete with a tablecloth, chinaware, and silver engraved with the captain's initials. It was all very grand and fancy. Alexander felt awkward in that he had never dined with anything other than pewter plates—not even at home, because his uncle had insisted that the good china be saved for company. Not that anyone ever came.

Magruder, who was the captain's orderly, seated the two ensigns side by side, farthest from the captain. Alexander wondered why two chairs were still empty, one next to him—and one closer up near the captain. He had his answer a moment later when the final three guests arrived. They all wore flyer uniforms, and as they came in, Alexander saw with pleasure that one of the new arrivals was Lord Parkington. He was given the chair next to Alexander, who was happy to see the flyer's face light up.

"If I must sit next to a sailor, I suppose you'll do," Parkington said, but the flyer was smiling as he said it. "It's good to see you up and about, by the way. I thought you had drowned. Leaping into the sea like that—it was outlandish. More like just the sort of thing to expect from a flyer, not a sailor. You're the ones who are supposed to have good sense, mind you."

Parkington introduced the other flyer, whose name was Thirwall. Like most of the young flyers, he was a slightly built boy. Too much weight would slow down a gryphon.

While the arrival of the two flyer ensigns was barely noticed, conversation dribbled to a halt as the third flyer officer approached the empty seat. Even Alexander couldn't help but stare.

Captain Bellingham leaped to his feet.

"Amelia, my dear, so glad you could join us," he said, his voice booming like cannon fire.

"Why thank you, Bellingham. It worked out very nicely having to fly in a message from fleet headquarters. I always do try to arrive in time for a good meal."

Bellingham laughed, and he seemed genuinely pleased to see the flyer officer. The other men didn't seem so sure, and they appeared very glad when Magruder set about refilling their wineglasses. They were all very hale and hearty about it, and Alexander detected a sense of relief that they had something else to focus upon.

Even Alexander was not immune to the tension caused by the flyer captain's arrival. She had clearly just flown in, because a smell of fresh salt air hung about her, along with a whiff of wet cat, that peculiar odor that gryphons had. He could smell it, too, on Lord Parkington, even though the boy was wearing his best uniform and hadn't just arrived by gryphon. The smell of gryphons seemed to permeate everything about the flyers.

But it was not the gryphon commander's smell that he noticed most of all—it was the jaunty air about her. The flyer captain was tall—taller than some of the men, though not as tall as Bellingham or as Professor Hobhouse. She was also willowy and lithe. She wore a heavy flying cloak against the cold, and Magruder helped her off with that, revealing a sky blue flyer's coat and riding breeches that hugged her curvy hips and shapely legs. Several of the men gulped at their wine.

"I believe all of you are acquainted with Amelia Blackburn—popularly known as Captain Amelia," Bellingham said. He smiled with what could only be described as fondness. "She is, of course, quite famous throughout the fleet."

"Oh, posh." Captain Amelia plunked down into the empty chair at the captain's elbow. "Magruder, pour me a generous glass. None of that namby pamby white there, but a nice deep port to get the chill out of my bones."

"Amelia, I think you in turn know everyone here, except our two more recent additions to the *Resolution*. Ensigns Higson and Hope."

Captain Amelia's gaze passed over Roger with barely any acknowledgment and then settled upon Alexander. "Hope, do you say?" She looked at the captain. "Not Arthur's son?"

"One and the same."

"Arthur Hope. Now there was a man." The gryphon commander sounded almost dreamy.

"Indeed," Bellingham agreed, with a tinge of sadness in his voice. "There was a man."

Alexander perked up at that, and yet he was unsettled. How could this woman possibly have known his father?

He might have asked, but at that moment

Magruder entered carrying a large silver tray on which there were three roasted chickens, surrounded by broiled potatoes and carrots. A general cheer went up, and Alexander's mouth watered at the smell. For the next several minutes, the only sound was the click and clatter of silverware and appreciative noises. Alexander spooned gravy over his potatoes and joined in. After a steady diet of ship's biscuit and boiled salt beef, he had almost forgotten how good real food tasted. He wolfed it down with relish.

Captain Amelia had taken a smaller portion than the men, and she only picked at that. She did have a second glass of port, however. The ensigns had been allowed a single, very small glass and Alexander found it to be a strong red wine, laced with brandy. He was not used to drinking wine, and only sipped at it. Everyone also had a goblet of water and mostly that's what he drank.

"What ho, Mr. Drury," the gryphon commander said to the sailing master, and raised her glass. "You're not keeping up."

The sailing master was already apple cheeked, but with a smile he held out his glass and Magruder refilled it with port wine.

When the general shoveling down of food had abated somewhat, conversation picked up again. "How did you fare in that gale?" Captain Amelia asked. "The entire gryphon flight was grounded for days. We couldn't launch in that wind. The only saving grace was that the Napoleonist gryphons couldn't fly, either."

"Truth be told, it was a close thing, Amelia," the captain said. "These winter storms that blow up on the channel are not to be taken lightly. In fact, we damn near lost Mr. Higson and Mr. Hope over the side."

"Oh?" She looked at the two ensigns with genuine interest. "Do tell."

"I was up in the rigging when one of the men lost his footing and ended up dragging me down with him," Roger explained. "It wasn't his fault, really. We would have drowned in that sea, if Alexander hadn't jumped in after us."

"You sailors always did have trouble with heights," Captain Amelia said.

"Damnedest thing I ever saw," said Mr. Drury, who was now positively red faced. "It was as if a wave picked them up and set them back on board. None the worse for wear, I might add, except for Ensign Hope, who promptly passed out."

"I'm sure it was a great shock to Mr. Hope's system," Lieutenant Swann seemed compelled to point out. "His actions were quite brave."

"Yet undeniably foolish," added Professor Hobhouse, who until then had been unusually quiet.

"Oh, Hobhouse, you always were such a one for gloom and doom and caution," Captain

Amelia said. Then, without warning, she picked up her goblet and hurled the water within it across the table at Alexander.

Without thinking, in a fraction of an instant, he willed the water to stop. And so it did, hanging suspended over the table. The officers around the table stared. Under the table, he felt Lord Parkington grab his knee. Suddenly conscious of what he had done, Alexander let the water splash onto the now-empty silver platter.

The sailing master was staring at the greasy puddle. "What in the world—"

"The boy is an elemental, of course," Captain Amelia said. "I wouldn't expect anything less from the son of Arthur Hope. Now, what sort of pudding do you suppose Magruder has made?"

CHAPTER 9

When Alexander woke the next morning, he was very glad to find himself in his own hammock in the ensigns' berth, rather than the one in the sick bay. He vaguely remembered crawling into his hammock last night, extremely sleepy and full from Captain Bellingham's dinner.

There was no sleeping late on a ship of war. The ensigns' berth was not a quiet place, and he realized that everyone around him was already awake. Roger's hammock was rolled up and stowed.

Alexander had gone to sleep fully clothed, though he had managed to kick off his shoes, and he now swung his bare feet toward the deck.

The first thing he saw was Thomas Fowler at

the table where the ensigns normally dined. From the mugs of coffee, biscuits and pots of jam, it looked as if they were having breakfast. Fowler was in the midst of a group of other ensigns and seemed to be telling a story that was funny enough to have them all laughing. Alexander was a little surprised because he had not thought of Fowler as much of a storyteller—unless the younger ensigns thought it was wise to laugh because Fowler wanted them to. Sweeney and Lloyd sat on either side of him like large bookends, snickering and casting looks in Alexander's direction.

"Don't pay him any mind," whispered Roger, who was nearby, sorting things in his sea chest. "It's just what he wants you to do."

"You there, Hopeless!" called Sweeney. "I hear you're allergic to saltwater. Makes you swoon like a girl, does it?"

Several boys looked in Alexander's direction. Some wore idiotic grins, and he realized that the story Fowler had been telling with such evident hilarity was about how Alexander had passed out on deck after being thrown back aboard *Resolution* by that rogue wave.

He felt a flash of anger, then pushed it aside. There was a burst of laughter from the table. They evidently found his silence hilarious. He busied himself putting on his shoes.

"What watch have you got?" asked Liam, who

plunked onto an empty sea chest, mug of steaming coffee in hand. He looked at Alexander. "What's wrong with you?"

"Fowler," Roger answered for him. "He's telling stories about Alexander fainting during the storm."

The Irish boy snorted. "That's not how I heard it. You should hear the men talking. They say you've got some sort of powers or magic, like a necromancer." He laughed. "Some are even saying you might be an elemental, like old Algernon Hope. They are a rather superstitious lot. They'll believe any old story. There are more than a few going around, including Fowler's over there."

Roger and Alexander exchanged a look. Roger had been there in the sea with him and knew how the wave had swept them back aboard the ship. More importantly, he had witnessed Captain Amelia's stunt last night with the hurled water. There was definitely something strange going on that Alexander didn't yet understand.

"Don't listen to Fowler," Liam muttered.

"You're not the one who passed out on deck," Alexander said.

With that, he stood up and walked over to the table. He could barely hear Roger whisper a warning after him. "Alexander, don't."

The laughter didn't quite die away as he walked up. The boys gathered around Fowler watched Alexander expectantly, wondering what he was about to say or do. There was nothing like a good fight to interrupt the boredom at sea. Fowler, who was much taller and older than Alexander, watched him approach with the sort of amused expression with which a cat regards a mouse.

"Good morning," Alexander said, then poured himself a mug of coffee.

He was so angry with Fowler and the others that his hands shook, but he hoped they didn't notice. He was determined not to let them see how their taunts ate at him. He grabbed a couple of biscuits to stuff in his pockets, then headed for the stairway.

"Careful there, Hopeless!" Fowler called after him. "We wouldn't want you to faint dead away at the sight of the sea this morning!"

Roger clapped Alexander on the shoulder, and Liam fell in behind them. He felt a little better knowing that not all of the ensigns found him to be a laughingstock—at least not the ones who mattered.

❊ ❊ ❊

The morning had started badly, even sullenly. The grayness of the winter day and the thought of watching the dull sea for hours did not help his mood. But in the next moment, everything changed.

They had just started up the gangway when the drums began to sound "Beat to Quarters." They could hear cries on deck of "All hands to action stations!" They flew up the ladder and emerged onto a deck in turmoil. This did not have the feel at all of a drill. There was a tang in the air of danger and anxiety, and yet Alexander could see no sign of any ships on the horizon. Then he looked up and felt his blood run cold.

It was a sight unlike any he had ever seen. In the distant sky he could see a formation like a "V" of geese, but this was no flock of migrating birds. They were larger and flew much more swiftly, pointed like an arrow at the *Resolution*. Alexander stood there, mesmerized.

"Are they ours?" he wondered out loud.

"Are you daft, boy?" a sailor replied, racing past with a bucket filled with loaded pistols. The small arms such as pistols and cutlasses were normally kept locked away to prevent mutiny, but now the sailor passed them to eager hands. He paused in front of Alexander. "Those are French gryphons! You'd better take a pistol, young sir—in point of fact, you ought to take two."

Alexander did just that, stuffing them into his belt as many of the men were doing. The sailor rushed away to arm other crew members. He felt better having a pair of pistols, though the gryphons soaring overhead seemed hopelessly beyond reach of a pistol shot. And if the French beasts were as large as Lord Parkington's gryphon, it would take more than a pistol to bring them down.

He could hear Lieutenant Swann shouting orders to the other officers and to the sailors. "Mr. Higson, see to your division! You there, belay that and fetch more powder!"

Alexander had not been on board long enough to be assigned a proper division, and so he did not have a task other than to make himself generally useful.

Most of the other ensigns were in charge of divisions—detachments of sailors who operated several of the ship's cannons. He could see Roger getting his men in order, and also Fowler, who seemed to have one of the larger divisions. As Alexander watched him direct his men, he had to give him some grudging respect because Fowler appeared to know what he was about. He also looked much calmer than Alexander felt at the moment. When Fowler gave an order, his men jumped to it.

Alexander had never been in a battle, and didn't know what to expect or how to act. He was surprised to find that he felt more confused than afraid. He just wished his first fight had involved another ship, rather than the terrifying enemy gryphons. How could a ship defend against an attack from the air?

From the talk he had heard, he knew that a gryphon attack was much feared. A ship at sea was in the open with nowhere to run and hide. The *Resolution's* massive guns could defend against another ship, but they were almost useless against gryphons because the guns could not be elevated to shoot straight into the sky.

For defense, a ship mainly had to rely on the marine sharpshooters in the rigging. Only their rifles and muskets had the range to reach the beasts. Alexander had heard that a swooping and flying gryphon was a notoriously difficult target to hit. A marksman had to be quick, and a good shot. And there was always the danger that a gryphon would simply dive down with claws and beak to snatch a man from the rigging.

To make matters worse, gryphon flyers carried spiked bomblets to rain down on deck, along with small explosive grenades. The beasts themselves were trained to shred the ship's sails with their claws, rendering a ship immobile.

The best way to fight back against a gryphon attack was to send the ship's own cohort of gryphons against it. The flyers—and the gryphons themselves—would attack each other in the air. At home, Alexander had sometimes seen hawks or birds fighting in the sky, and he expected something like that.

Almost as soon as he thought it, he heard a

great thud come from below. He leaned over the rail and saw that *Resolution's* gryphon port had been lowered, and one by one the ship's gryphons sprang off the flight deck, riders clinging to their saddles. Some had clearly just tumbled out of their hammocks and hadn't put on their coats; one rider went barefoot. When scouting or flying messages, a flyer usually went alone, but for combat, there were two flyers aboard each gryphon—a pilot and a stern rider. He wondered if this might slow down the beasts, but he soon understood why two flyers were better than one.

Sweeping in from the sea, the Napoleonist squadron was now close enough for Alexander to make out the individual riders, who wore the elaborate uniform of Napoleon's famed cavalry, the cuirassiers: high black boots that went above the knee, gleaming white breeches, blue coat with red epaulets. Each French flyer wore a metal cuirass—armor that protected the chest and back. They wore helmets topped with horsehair that streamed behind them in the wind. The gryphons had armor plating shined to a mirror finish as well as saddle blankets in pale blue trimmed with gold. The French might have looked gaudy if they hadn't been so terrifying. In comparison, the English gryphons and half-dressed flyers resembled a motley flock of pigeons. Overhead, a horn sounded the Napoleonist attack, and Alexander felt his legs turn to jelly.

The enemy gryphons were upon them like a gust of wind. The marines fired a volley, the sound of cracking muskets filling the air. One vaguely red-tinted beast swept through the rigging and clawed at the marine snipers, causing two of them to fall. They spun through the air, flailing and screaming, then landed on deck with a sickening thud. Alexander stared in horror at the broken lumps that had once been seemingly invincible marines.

The *Resolution's* own gryphons were just getting airborne, and a pair of French gryphons ripped through their formation, scattering them in all directions. Alexander groaned. He couldn't tell which flyer and gryphon might be Lord Parkington and Lemondrop, but he hoped they would be all right.

"Take cover!" someone shouted, and Alexander looked up to see a shower of glittering objects falling toward the sailors. He stared, mesmerized, at what looked like shimmering rain coming down. Then he felt himself roughly grabbed and discovered it was none other than Captain Bellingham, who held Alexander by the collar as he raised a round wooden shield above their heads. Instantly, there was a thunk, thunk sound as the razor-sharp bomblets cut into the wood, but the shield stopped them as effectively as an umbrella stops the rain.

"You might try to move a bit more quickly next time, Mr. Hope," said the captain. "It doesn't do to watch the bomblets coming down, pretty as they look, because it may very well be the last sight you see."

Like Alexander, some of the sailors had been too slow, and the bomblets had caught them with devastating results, slashing through arms, shoulders and scalps. Several men now lay sprawled on the deck, bloodied and groaning. Captain Bellingham lowered the shield and was gone, marching down the deck shouting orders. Alexander marveled that the captain had very likely just saved his life, as casually as if he had helped him down from a carriage.

Several of the enemy gryphons circled back after the bomblet attack. Some dived through the rigging to harass the Marine snipers, while others landed directly on *Resolution's* spars and sails. The gryphons clawed at the canvas and the French riders hacked at the lines and pulleys with swords and boarding axes. Great slashes appeared in the sails.

The *Resolution* was far from helpless. Alexander heard Lieutenant Jones of the marines shout "Fire!" and another volley ripped out. A single French flyer toppled from his saddle and plunged into the sea like a falling stone. The enemy gryphon was unharmed, and circled the ship with angry cries, seemingly unsure what to do without its rider. On deck, sailors aimed their pistols at the gryphons, but the French were mostly out of range or flew so swiftly that they were almost impossible to hit.

It was their own flyers who had the most telling effect on the Napoleonists, engaging them in air-to-air combat. As Alexander watched, two gryphons charged each other and nearly collided mid-air. The gryphons reared back, held in place by their enormous beating wings, clawing at each other with their hind legs. Swords clanged as the flyers fought. There was something familiar about the British pilot, and then he realized the flyer was Captain Amelia. Her sword flashed again and again as she attacked the enemy flyer. He wondered what the Frenchman must think, discovering that he was fighting a woman.

The French gryphons had just one rider each, indicating that they must have flown a great distance as rapidly as possible. Alexander could quickly see the advantage of two riders. One flyer piloted the gryphon and attacked or defended from the front, while the stern rider defended against attacks that came from another direction, or fired shots at the enemy. It was a strategy that made the Royal Navy gryphons a formidable foe.

Overhead, Alexander watched the two gryphons locked in combat as they rolled and grappled, trying for the advantage, all the while screaming their deafening battle cries. Like war eagles, he thought. He saw Captain Amelia's sword flicker quick as lightning and then the Frenchman went limp in the saddle. The enemy gryphon gave a final cry of defeat before flying off with the wounded flyer slumped across the beast's neck. On deck, others had been watching Captain Amelia's duel with the French flyer, and a cheer went up from the sailors.

The Napoleonists were not defeated. Far from it. A fresh wave of bomblets rained down, and this time Alexander dived beneath one of the cannons on deck. The bomblets tinged harmlessly against the iron barrel, but elsewhere on deck the sharp spikes found their mark and sailors cried out in agony.

He got back to his feet. Everywhere that Alexander looked, the enemy gryphons seemed to be tearing the *Resolution* to shreds. As he watched, a French gryphon settled high in the rigging and began biting at the lines and tackle.

"Dear God, he'll leave us helpless!" Captain Bellingham cried. "Someone shoot that devil-beak!"

Several pistols popped, but the gryphon was too high above the deck for the balls to have any effect. But then a British gryphon swept in and Alexander could see that it was Lemondrop, piloted by Lord Parkington. The Frenchman leveled a blunderbuss at Lemondrop and there was a burst of flame and smoke. Alexander held his breath.

Lemondrop veered away, apparently unhurt, but one of the British flyers was not so lucky. The stern rider slumped in the saddle, badly wounded by the blast. It's very likely he would have fallen if he hadn't been securely strapped in. Lord Parkington and Lemondrop hadn't been hit. Alexander remembered to breathe again.

He turned his attention back to the deck, wondering how he could help. The battle seemed to be taking place high above, beyond his reach. The screeching battle cries of the gryphons had become so awful that he wanted to cover his ears.

Just when it seemed the situation couldn't be any worse, someone shouted: "Sail ahoy!"

Already, several of the sailors were pointing in that direction. Alexander could make out a ship bearing down of them under full sail. The enemy ship was smaller than the *Resolution*, but with her sails sliced to ribbons and flapping uselessly, *Resolution* would be fighting with one hand behind her back. These were just the tactics Alexander had been warned about: an aerial assault to render the ship unable to sail properly, and then an ambush by a ship or ships that had been lurking just out of sight. The Napoleonist ship was still very far away, but it would be here soon enough.

Even with damaged sails, this was an enemy that a British ship of the line could defend against. Sailors ran to their battle stations, rolling out guns and clearing the deck for action. Then another wave of bomblets came down upon the heads of the unsuspecting sailors, creating more chaos on deck.

Alexander was still trying to figure out what to do with himself when he was astonished to find the deck beside him suddenly filled with a gryphon. One minute the deck had been empty, and then the gryphon had landed lightly as a cat. The rush of wind from the wings, however, almost knocked him over. He slipped and nearly fell. He realized, horrified, that he had lost his footing because there was blood on the deck. The French bomblets had had a telling effect.

"Take him off! He's badly hurt!"

Alexander recognized Lord Parkington's shrill, commanding voice. Several sailors rushed forward to help the wounded stern rider out of the saddle. Alexander recognized the hurt flyer, but did not know his name. He appeared to be unconscious.

"Mr. Hope, get on!" Now his lordship was shouting directly at him.

"What?"

"Are you deaf? I need a stern rider, and Benson there is out of commission. Come on!"

Even in the midst of the battle and the carnage on deck, Alexander might have argued. But as he stepped closer to the gryphon, several hands caught him and lifted him onto the gryphon's back. He swung one leg over the saddle. Someone strapped him in and he recognized Jameson, who was one of the few men tall enough to reach that high. "Good luck, sir," he said as the heavy brass buckle clicked into place.

"Better take these, sir!" A pair of loaded pistols was thrust at him, and he stuck them through his belt. Then someone gave him a cutlass. He tossed his bi-corn hat to Jameson for safekeeping.

"More guns!" Parkington cried. "Doesn't anyone else have a pistol?"

Alexander grabbed at the pistols being offered up, and either jammed them through his belt or into his boots. He slung the cutlass and scabbard over his shoulder. The air around them was filled with the cries of war gryphons and injured men, punctuated by the crack of muskets. Overhead, the enemy gryphons had reformed and were coming again to pelt the *Resolution* with bomblets. Lord Parkington must have seen them, because he shouted at Alexander to hang on, and then gave Lemondrop's reins a shake.

Alexander felt the gryphon's muscular rear legs tense beneath him, and the next thing he knew the deck fell away and they rushed upward past the *Resolution's* rigging fast as an arrow, driven higher and higher by the gryphon's powerful wings.

Alexander gripped his saddle in utter fear. Beneath them, the *Resolution* was now the size of a toy boat. At a command from Parkington, Lemondrop stopped climbing and beat his wings in the same way someone might tread water to stay afloat. After the rush of wind in his ears, it was oddly quiet as the gryphon treaded air. They were above the formation of enemy gryphons bearing down on the ship.

"We're going to dive right through them," Parkington shouted. "Get your pistols out. You'll only have time for a shot or two."

The thought of what they were about to do terrified Alexander. "How am I supposed to hang on with pistols in my hands?"

"You're not going anywhere as long as you're strapped into the saddle."

"What the devil will you be doing?" Alexander asked.

"Flying." He kicked his heels into Lemondrop's sides the same way that someone would urge a horse to gallop. "Now!"

Alexander's stomach lurched sickeningly as the gryphon plummeted toward the enemy gryphons. Alexander was as terrified as he had ever been, and he fought the urge to toss away the pistols and hang onto the saddle for dear life. Down below he glimpsed the *Resolution*, helplessly waiting as the enemy gryphons approached. This was his ship now, his home, his corner of

England. The thought that the Napoleonists were intent on attacking the ship filled him with outrage. He cocked the pistols and gave a wild war cry that the wind threw back at him.

Lemondrop shot down like an arrow and wind shrieked in Alexander's ears. All at once, the sea loomed closer. This was madness, but the sheer terror of it all was somehow thrilling as they shot toward the French formation. At the last instant, Lemondrop rotated to come at them with his talons. The lurching stop nearly tore Alexander from his saddle. They swept among the squadron, catching them by surprise. Lemondrop swiped at a French gryphon and drew blood.

Alexander raised the pistols and fired wildly at the nearest French flyer, too excited to take aim. He was so close that he could see the Frenchman's mustache and the look of surprise on his face. The shots missed, but he made the French flyer duck and pull back on the reins, causing his gryphon to fall out of formation.

And then they were suddenly below the French and racing away. They were too badly outnumbered to stay and fight, but they had singlehandedly caused the enemy attack to fall apart. Alexander heard cheering from the deck of *Resolution*.

The Napoleonists were not going to let them get away unpunished. They were stirred up as madly as hornets. One of the gryphons broke away from the remnants of the French formation and rushed toward them with powerful bursts of the beast's wings. Even from a distance, Alexander could see that it was the gryphon and flyer at whom he had emptied his pistols.

"They're after us!" he warned.

"I'll try to lose them," his lordship shouted above the wind. "You guard the rear."

Lemondrop hurtled toward the ship and suddenly rotated so that one wingtip pointed toward the sea, the other at the sky. Alexander found himself flying sideways and was thankful that he was strapped in. The maneuver allowed the gryphon to slip neatly between the masts. Musket fire cracked and Alexander worried that the *Resolutions* had mistakenly fired at them, but realized that they were aiming for the French gryphon on their tail.

They swept away from the ship and Alexander glanced back to see the enemy gryphon still bearing down upon them.

Parkington saw it too. "By Jupiter, they're fast!" he cried. He handed back a pistol. "Give them a taste of lead and see if that doesn't slow them down!"

Alexander took aim, struggling to steady the pistol. He fired at the Frenchman's head, but his shot went wide.

"I swear you bloody sailors couldn't hit a target the size of Buckingham Palace with a pistol!"

Lord Parkington cried. "Hang on!"

Lemondrop dove toward the sea at a speed that threatened to rip Alexander's hair out by the roots. Just when it seemed they were about to crash into the waves, they pulled up and skimmed along so close to the water that Alexander's boots got wet. Behind them, a pistol cracked and a bullet zipped audibly between them. The French gryphon seemed to be gaining.

"He's closer!" Alexander shouted. Try as they might, they couldn't seem to shake off the Napoleonist. The enemy flyer was raising another pistol and Alexander had the helpless feeling that he or Lemondrop were in the sights.

"Now, do it now, Alexander!" Lord Parkington cried.

"What?" He was confused. He had no weapons left except the sword, which was useless at that distance.

"Why do you think I flew us so close to the sea? Use your power!"

It was impossible. Alexander's heart hammered and he could barely think. He looked back at the Frenchman and saw that he had raised a second pistol, so that he was now holding one in each hand. The enemy gryphon was very swift and had gained on them until Alexander could see a grin of triumph on the French flyer's face. He couldn't miss at that range.

"Mr. Hope, sometime today would be helpful!"

Lord Parkington's voice was shrill, almost pleading.

He closed his eyes, then dipped his foot out of the stirrup until it just touched the waves. If he lowered his foot any further, the force of the water would rip him from the saddle, harness or not. In his mind's eye, he imagined the spray from his boot whirling in the wind ... joining together in a long stream of water ... whipping around and hitting the Frenchman like a hose ...

Nothing.

And then in frustration, Alexander willed a wave to leap up like a wall.

Behind them, they heard a cry. Alexander opened his eyes to see the enemy gryphon smashing into the rogue wave. Flyer and gryphon toppled into the sea.

Lemondrop swerved upward and spun round, flying back over the Frenchman. He and his gryphon appeared to be extremely wet but unhurt. Gryphons were strong swimmers, much like horses, and as long as the Frenchman stayed on the beast's back he would be fine. The Frenchman shook a fist at them. Lemondrop, Lord Parkington and Alexander flew toward *Resolution*.

The Napoleonist attack was broken. The *Resolution's* gryphons had rallied and driven them off, with help from the steady fire by the marine sharpshooters. Lemondrop was the last gryphon to return, and they were greeted by cheering from the deck as they swept overhead.

Alexander's head throbbed dully, but he still managed to wave. If this was victory, he thought, it tasted awfully sweet.

He fumbled with the big brass buckles of the harness and managed to undo them, then swung down off Lemondrop. It felt terribly good to feel the solid wooden deck beneath his feet.

"Look!" someone shouted. "They're coming back!"

He looked skyward and saw that a handful of the French beasts had reformed into an attack formation, though there weren't as many as there had been. They formed a dark wedge against the sky, and he thought he had never seen anything so sinister.

Even from a distance, he could see the telltale sacks of bomblets hanging from the beasts' sides. And there was a new threat—the enemy gryphons seemed to be trailing smoke. They would be dropping incendiary bombs. Fire was a terrible threat to a wooden ship. The Napoleonists had saved the worst for last. He felt his joy at what he thought was victory melt like a lump of sugar in hot tea.

The enemy retreat must have been a feint engineered to catch them off guard. It had worked splendidly. The marine sharpshooters were already climbing down from the rigging, muskets slung over their shoulders. Several of the gryphons already had landed and were unsaddled in the gryphon port. Lemondrop was the only British gryphon on deck that still had a flyer in the saddle. Without waiting for Alexander to return to the saddle, Lord Parkington launched Lemondrop into the sky with a tremendous leap.

Lemondrop was a powerful and enormously fast gryphon, and he hurtled toward the French, scattering their formation. Lord Parkington's sword flashed, and one of the enemy beasts went spinning away, crying in pain, and turned toward the French coast. That still left four against one, and they quickly counterattacked. Pistols cracked and swords gleamed as the enemy came at Lemondrop. Watching from deck, Alexander could only watch helplessly.

"They'll shred 'em to pieces!" cried one sailor, aghast.

More shots rang out. Then Parkington slumped in the saddle. Without thinking, Alexander cried: "No!"

Sensing victory, the Napoleonists descended on the British gryphon and wounded flyer. Lemondrop rolled and dodged, trying to save himself and his flyer. With a burst of speed, he broke free of his attackers and rose higher and higher, trying to get above them, all the while headed away from the ship as if to draw off the attackers.

The last glimpse Alexander had of Lemondrop was a tiny dot against the gray sky, pulling away from the pursuing enemy gryphons.

Headed toward the French coast.

CHAPTER 10

The officers of *Resolution* had gathered in Captain Bellingham's cabin. Night had fallen, so that the room was lighted by gently swaying lanterns and candles. The faces illuminated here should have been happy, or relieved at the very least, because the ship had survived a fierce attack early that morning.

Fortunately, the small Napoleonist ship had turned tail and fled after a full broadside from the frigate, having discovered that *Resolution* still had plenty of fight in her. The rest of the day had been spent repairing damage, tending the wounded, and otherwise setting things right. The group standing before the captain was grim-faced and quiet rather than content.

Alexander wasn't quite sure why he was there —none of the other naval ensigns were—but he had found himself grabbed by the arm and almost forcibly marched there by none other than Captain Amelia.

"We've lost Parkington and Lemondrop," the flyer captain said without preamble, now that the meeting had begun. A fresh bandage gleamed white against her temple where a French sword had nicked her. "And we should like to get them back."

"Get them back from where?" the ship's captain asked. He added gently, "Amelia, they must have gone down and been lost at sea."

"We've been flying patrols," she said. "Wider and wider rings each time. There's no sign of them on the sea. If they were there, my Desdemona would have seen them. Believe me. They must have reached France."

"What do you expect me to do?" The captain's voice sounded tense and angry. "I lost ten good men today due to those damned Napoleonists and their bomblets. There are another twenty in the surgery being treated by the surgeon and Professor Hobhouse."

"You sea-lubbers weren't the only ones with losses today," Captain Amelia snapped back, sounding every bit as angry as Bellingham. "Mr. Rigley and Able Airman Hazel launched with the gryphon named Biscuit to meet the surprise attack by the French beasts. They engaged the enemy and Able Airman Hazel fell during the air battle."

Alexander was struck by the term "fell," which sounded so noble compared to the reality of the boy's death. He had heard from the other flyers that Able Airman Hazel—who had turned seventeen two weeks ago—had been hit by a lucky shot from a Napoleonist pistol and his restraining harness had given way as he slumped in the saddle. His body had then pinwheeled several hundred feet before plummeting into the sea. The bullet may or may not have been fatal, but the plunge into the sea definitely had *killed* him, to put it less poetically.

Bellingham nodded silently. It was unsaid, but he was in a difficult position. Though they were of equal rank, Bellingham technically commanded *Resolution* and all those aboard. Although she was not attached to the ship, having come there bearing messages from fleet command, Captain Amelia by privilege of rank not only commanded all flyers and gryphons aboard but now spoke for them.

"You ask a great deal of me, Amelia."

"I know you'll do the right thing, Bellingham. This is one of your crew. A British flyer and gryphon in danger of being captured by the French."

There was silence at the implications of that.

The thought of a Royal Navy flyer and gryphon falling into Napoleonist hands was almost too terrible to contemplate. It was well known that a captured flyer found alone on French soil might be treated like a spy rather than a proper soldier. That meant he could be hanged or shot.

And then there was the treatment of captured gryphons. Gryphons were more loyal and intelligent than horses or even dogs, so it was believed a gryphon that had trained closely with one flyer never could be completely trusted with another—especially if that flyer was French. There were rumors that the Napoleonists kept captured gryphons for breeding, but that they cut off their wings so that they could never return home to help the English. It was a cruelty almost too awful to contemplate.

Captain Amelia broke the silence. "Well," she said. "It's quite clear that we shall have to go after them."

"What? Fly into France after one flyer and gryphon? That's madness, Amelia!"

"Come now, Bellingham. I would have thought you'd see it as a matter of duty."

Off to one side, the sailing master began to sputter in much the same way that a lid clatters on a boiling pot. "A horse has better sense than a gryphon," he said. "At least a horse will return to its stable rather than fly into enemy territory!"

Captain Amelia regarded him coldly. "I can

assure you, Mr. Drury, that a gryphon is not a horse. And if I recall, *Resolution* was under severe attack at the time. Lemondrop knew to lead the attackers away from us, toward the coast."

"The French coast!" Mr. Drury, done with sputtering, nearly shouted. "Not bloody England!"

"A gryphon is a beast, Mr. Drury," the flyer captain responded. "A clever beast, to be sure, but not one that's particularly able to reason or do sensible things. Lemondrop was following his instincts to protect the ship and his flyer."

The sailing master puffed up his wide cheeks, ready to respond, but the captain stopped him with a wave of his hand. "Belay that, if you please, Mr. Drury. We'll make no headway in debating the faults and merits of gryphons. What do you propose, Amelia?"

"A rescue mission."

The naval officers exchanged glances, but knew better than to speak up before the captain. What was unsaid was that a rescue mission into French territory was highly irregular. But that was a flyer for you. Always doing the unconventional. And Captain Amelia made most flyers look dull as a country vicar by comparison.

"What an interesting proposal," the ship's captain said.

"Think of the audacity of it, Bellingham. We'll be operating under the very noses of the French.

We'll take two gryphons into France," she said. "Mr. Hope and myself on Desdemona. Mr. Rigley on Biscuit, one of our strongest flyers."

What Bellingham said next surprised Alexander. "Why on earth do you want Mr. Hope?"

Alexander might have asked the same question. It was no secret that Alexander had done well flying with Parkington on Lemondrop. But he wasn't so sure he wanted to fly clear to France.

"He is Lord Parkington's closest friend on this ship and he's not bad in the air. From what I can see, he's still too green to be of much use on your ship." She paused. "But he has certain skills that may be useful."

"Parlor tricks, Amelia! Nelson's hat, but this mission you've proposed is truly madness." Captain Bellingham clasped his hands behind his back and paced. The small, crowded room was confining, so that he resembled a tiger in a cage. "I don't know. If things go wrong the French will have gained a Flyer captain and two more of our gryphons. It seems a bad trade to me for a wounded ensign and a gryphon, if you forgive me for saying so."

"I shall, though your practical nature at times smacks of cruelty toward Lord Parkington," the flyer captain said. Several eyebrows went up in the cabin, but Bellingham seemed nonplussed. A silence fell around the room. The captain's words had had the ring of finality, but Amelia had hinted that she had yet to play her trump card. It was well known around the fleet that Captain Amelia held aristocratic titles in contempt and used them grudgingly, even with her superiors. She avoided calling Parkington anything other than "mister," as if he were nothing more than a lowly adolescent ensign.

"I believe that will be all, Amelia," the captain said.

"Not quite, Bellingham. Let me point out that Lord Parkington may be a mere boy, but he is cousin to the king," she said quietly, as if she and Bellingham were the only two in the room. "Do you think King George would wish his young cousin to be a hostage and prisoner of the French? Napoleon would like nothing better than to use him as a pawn in this game of kings and emperors, or hang him as a spy to thumb his Gallic nose at the English throne. Let us bring him back among friends."

Captain Bellingham thought about it for several long moments, and then slowly nodded. "Very well then. But you shall also take Professor Hobhouse."

"Why in the name of Jupiter would I do that? We're going to rescue an earl, not conjugate verbs or do long division."

"Hobhouse speaks fluent French," Bellingham

said, as if it was perfectly obvious. A slight smile crossed his face the way a ripple of wind might cause a sail to dance. "Whatever shall you do if you need to stop and ask directions?"

❋ ❋ ❋

They spent the next few hours making preparations for the mission into France. Alexander made several trips around the ship, gathering items as commanded by Captain Amelia. A cold rain had sprung up, driven by a gusty wind across the English Channel. Alexander was soon soaked to the skin. It did not seem like promising weather for a secret mission into France, but the flyer who would be accompanying them was reassuring about the rain.

"A gryphon can fly in almost any weather short of a full-blown gale," Rigley said. "My Biscuit and Captain Amelia's Desdemona are two of the best creatures there are with two wings. And dirty weather like this will keep the French lookouts from spotting us, so that works in our favor."

Alexander's errands kept him too busy to think much, but he had to agree with Captain Bellingham that flying into French territory seemed liked madness. Yet Captain Amelia sounded confident enough, as if this were no more than a message run between ships in the fleet. Never mind that they had been busy gathering pistols and having the armorer sharpen their cutlasses. Following Captain Amelia's orders, Alexander also had fetched a quantity of bandages from the ship's surgeon and packed them in a waterproof saddlebag.

A cloaked figure appeared above as Alexander climbed a ladder toward the upper deck. He nearly fell when a boot stamped on his hand. Alexander looked up irritably. It was Fowler, who was coming off his watch on deck.

"Look where you're going, Hopeless!" Fowler said, a nasty smile on his face. "I've just heard about your little mission to save his lordship. I wouldn't give a brass farthing for your chances, considering you can't seem to make your way around the ship without coming to harm."

"Do try to keep the rum barrels safe while I'm in France," Alexander said.

"You'll forgive me if I don't wish you luck," Fowler said, shaking the rain off his coat and into Alexander's face before climbing the rest of the way down the ladder. "I'm sure some French cuirassier is going to gut you like a fish as soon as you touch down. What a pity."

Alexander was still gnashing his teeth when he found Roger bundling himself in a foul weather cloak on his way to his shift on watch. Roger took him by the arm urgently. "Alexander! I've been looking all over for you but I just now have to go on watch. I'm glad I found you! I just wanted to wish you luck, and hope that you get Lord Parky back here in once piece. Those bloody flyers are so much trouble. It just figures that it takes a good sailor to rescue them!"

Alexander was so touched that it was all he could do to mumble, "Thank you, Roger," before continuing on his way.

Once they had everything assembled and packed, Alexander was bone tired. But he expected he would be far too excited—and anxious—to get much sleep. He was already uneasy, and it didn't help that Amelia wanted him to sleep in the gryphon deck.

"Stick with Rigley. I don't want to have to track you down among all those sleeping ensigns," she informed him, and then wrinkled her nose. "You boys are a smelly bunch, I might add, stinking up your quarters with dirty stockings and bean farts."

Alexander was a bit embarrassed. There was a certain funk that hung about the ensigns' quarters. He might have said the same about the gryphon deck. The smells here were so foreign. Unlike the cramped ensigns' quarters, there was plenty of fresh air from several open ports. The gryphons preferred the smell of open sky. Alexander was already wet through from running errands in the cold rain to get ready for the mission, and he soon found himself shivering as he followed Rigley toward Biscuit's stall.

While the air was cool and fresh, the smell of the gryphons themselves was unnerving. Like horses, the beasts had their own peculiar scent. It was more lion than cat, both feline and feral. The smell was something he might never get used to, at least not for one night. He also soon realized that unlike the ensigns' berth, there were no hammocks.

"Where do you sleep?" he asked, looking around.

"I sleep in the stall with Biscuit," Rigley explained. He offered a conspiratorial grin. "Warmest place on the ship."

Alexander took one look at Biscuit, who appeared calm enough, but gazed at him with the unsettling stare that a cat might use on a mouse. Each gryphon was different. He recalled that Lemondrop was built lean and long as a thoroughbred racehorse, making him extremely fast. Biscuit was heavy and lumpy as his name implied, somewhat ungainly on deck, but a very powerful beast in the air. The sheer size of him tended to intimidate the French gryphons.

"Won't he roll over and crush you?"

"No, and neither would a horse, you ninny, and gryphons are much smarter and more attached to their flyers." Rigley paused, as if considering something. "There's room for you, if you wish. It will save time in the morning. Otherwise, you'll probably get lost down here or oversleep and we'll have to hunt you up."

He looked around. There *was* a nice warmth. A lantern gave off a dim light, and the stall was lined with fresh straw. It was almost cozy—and definitely more spacious than what either the ensigns or the sailors might expect. "All right," he said. "As long as you promise your devil-beak doesn't get hungry during the night and have me for a treat."

"You'd be a bit too stringy for his tastes, I'd wager. Not nearly enough meat on your bones for him."

Alexander rolled himself in a blanket. To his horror, Rigley lay down next to the beast.

"Good night," he said.

"Good night," Alexander answered. He had expected to have trouble sleeping, here in these strange quarters, among the beasts. He thought he would have missed his hammock. He also knew he should have been afraid for an entirely different reason—not because of the gryphons but because they would by flying into enemy territory tomorrow. Instead, Alexander found that he was excited. That alone might have kept him awake, but all at once the warmth enveloped him and exhaustion stole through him. He closed his eyes and slept.

CHAPTER 11

It only seemed like minutes later that they were roused in the dark by Captain Amelia herself. Alexander had slept in his clothes again—he scarcely remembered what it was like not to—and he reached for his boots and pulled them on. The flyers' steward came around with coffee and biscuits, but Alexander waved him off. The gryphons were being fed chunks of raw meat—the sight and smell of fresh blood would have taken away Alexander's appetite if he hadn't already been too nervous to eat. Then the gryphons were saddled. They were traveling light, taking nothing other than their weapons and medical supplies. They filled the remaining space in their saddlebags with bread and flasks of water.

When it came time to climb aboard Desdemona, Alexander was still so groggy with sleep that he fumbled with the brass buckles.

"Oh for heaven's sake, Mr. Hope!" Captain Amelia cried in exasperation, so that one of the flyer crew members hurried over to help strap Alexander into his long distance flying harness. They then rigged up the speaking tube, which made for easier communication on long flight, eliminating the need to yell at each other over the roar of the wind.

He glanced over at Professor Hobhouse and Rigley on board Biscuit. Rigley was old to be a mere flyer ensign, but Alexander had learned that there were ensigns like him who wanted nothing more than to fly. He had no interest in commanding his own squadron someday. Rigley had a reputation for being one of the best gryphon pilots in the fleet, though he was something of a daredevil. There was a gleam in his eye that showed he couldn't wait to get in the air. Professor Hobhouse looked rather pale and drawn, but resolute. He was so tall that he looked out of place, even on Biscuit, one of the larger gryphons. Once up on Biscuit's broad back, he had to stay hunched over to keep from cracking his noggin against the beams overhead.

The gryphon port was already open to the gray morning and cold sea air washed in, smelling strongly of salt. The ship had come about so that the gryphon port opened into the wind to make the launch easier, but being broadside to the waves made the ship roll heavily.

Alexander could hear the waves lurching against *Resolution*, and he found himself reaching out, willing the waves to quiet themselves. Nothing seemed to happen, other than the telltale beginnings of a headache. Alexander forgot about the waves and put his mind to other things, such as getting a good grip on the saddle horn. Unlike the so-called "English" saddles that most horse riders used, gryphon saddles were deep enough to grip the rider and had a horn that one might hold onto for balance when, say, swinging a sword at the enemy.

"Goggles on, if you please, Mr. Hope," said Captain Amelia, then guided Desdemona out the gryphon port and onto the wide wooden launch platform. The flyer captain stood for a moment and scratched Desdemona's ears. The gryphon nuzzled Amelia in return and made a nickering sound deep in her throat, almost like a horse. Compared with the other gryphons aboard *Resolution*, he had noticed that Desdemona was smaller than the others—built more like a panther than a lion, lithe and quick. But she was still strong enough to carry them both. "That's a good girl. We're in for a long flight and a bit of dodgy business if we meet a squadron of the enemy."

Looking on, Alexander was struck by the obvious connection between the flyer commander and her gryphon. He had thought of Amelia as harsh, but what he was watching was a private scene of tenderness between the gryphon and the flyer captain—and Amelia didn't seem to know that she was being watched. Then she climbed aboard the gryphon.

The wind whistled here on the launch deck, and the gray waves below looked hungry. Alexander gulped. Desdemona seemed to coil herself on her powerful hind legs. She sprang forward and suddenly there was no longer a wooden platform beneath them but only the waves, coming up at them fast.

Desdemona stretched out her wings and caught the wind. The gryphon gained altitude and with a few beats of her wings rose high above the ship. Below them, Biscuit took to the air in much the same way. He was a great, heavy beast —a sort of gryphon version of a Clydesdale—and had to beat his wings much harder to get aloft. Alexander felt dizzy as he watched the ship grow smaller far below.

He wasn't sure how many times it would take him to get used to riding a gryphon, if he ever did. He was quickly learning that it was neither the heights nor the stomach-churning aerial maneuvers that bothered him much. It was the sense of not being in control. He had come to realize that he didn't particularly like being a stern rider aboard a gryphon because he was, after all, just along for the ride.

Captain Amelia had other ideas.

"Keep a sharp eye out, Mr. Hope," she said into the speaking tube. "There will be enemy patrols that we wish to avoid."

It turned out that *Resolution* had been cruising just beyond sight of the French coast. The two gryphons flew so swiftly that the shoreline soon came into view. Alexander hardly knew what to think. All his life he had been taught that the French were the enemy. At the same time, France had seemed so distant from the woods and fields around Kingston Hall that it may as well have been the moon. Now here was France on the horizon, growing closer every moment.

Desdemona was very swift, being a messenger gryphon, and Captain Amelia guided her expertly to catch every favorable eddy of the air. He had the distinct impression that Biscuit was lumbering along heavily, puffing with the effort of keeping up with the swifter gryphon, and that Desdemona was holding back in order that they might fly in together.

They soon saw the white surf line of the coast, then dunes, then trees. The gryphons swept in low over the fields. Even over the rush of wind in his ears, Alexander thought he could hear Desdemona sniffing the air.

To think that Lord Parkington and Lemondrop were out there somewhere in all the vast country that lay ahead made finding them seem all that much more impossible. Alexander imagined his friend somewhere on that coast, lying wounded, or perhaps already a prisoner of the Napoleonists. The thought made him shudder. Captain Amelia had bragged that Desdemona was a good tracker, but they would also have to be extremely lucky.

Gryphons are unique in that they have the highly developed sense of smell of a lion, but also an eagle's keen vision. Desdemona's eyes were now so intent that they seemed to cut through the mist below like a torch.

At first glance, the woods and fields could have been England, not unlike the ones Alexander had explored as a young boy. A closer look revealed something distinctly different about the landscape. Something foreign. From the air, the French countryside was a patchwork of fields separated by massive hedgerows and stone walls. Country lanes wove through like the seams of a quilt. The farm houses here had thatched roofs like the ones in England, but the buildings themselves were made of stone and lower to the ground, unlike the whitewashed, story-and-a-half cottages of England.

A few farmers worked in the fields, appearing as little dabs of gray and white fabric. They scarcely noticed gryphons anymore because this area near the coast would be patrolled constantly, the skies dotted with the passing of messenger and sentry gryphons.

While the French farmers gave them scarcely any notice, it was these enemy gryphons that they were most worried about, lest they raise the alarm. While Desdemona and Captain Amelia scanned the countryside, the other gryphon piloted by Rigley and carrying Professor Hobhouse hung slightly back and above, keeping an eye on the skies.

"There!" Amelia shouted through the speaking tube. "French cavalry!" She pointed down, and Alexander spotted a file of horsemen passing along one of the muddy roads. Even in the gloomy light he could see their armor and steel helmets glinting, marking them as the dreaded cuirassiers of Napoleon's army.

"What should we do?" Alexander shouted back. They were traveling light and had no bomblets or anything useful for attacking the cuirassiers, just pistols and swords.

"Nothing," Amelia said. "With luck, they shan't even notice us."

Amelia was right. If the cavalry even paid them any mind, they would take the British gryphons for a French patrol. Still, Alexander couldn't help but think they were on borrowed time. Two British gryphons couldn't fly for long in the French skies before they were noticed, and then there would be trouble. Meanwhile, it seemed to Alexander that they were searching for the proverbial needle in a haystack, albeit a French one. There were no clues, no trail to follow. What had seemed this morning like a daring rescue mission now felt like a fool's errand. He felt his heart sink.

They flew for nearly an hour, searching in larger and larger circles. Nothing. Just brown, wintry countryside. Three times they had to duck into drifting cloud banks to escape detection by passing French couriers.

"We've come too far," Captain Amelia announced via the speaking tube. "We'll circle our way back to the coast."

Amelia signaled Rigley, and together the two gryphons worked over a new grid of woods, fields and farms, slightly south of their first search zone.

"What if they were captured?" Alexander couldn't resist asking. "There's no way we could know that."

"Maybe they were captured, or maybe they're wounded and hiding out under a hedgerow," Amelia said. "We've come this far, and I'm not giving up yet. Now stop distracting me with silly questions, Mr. Hope, and let us focus our attention on the search."

The flyer captain hadn't said it, but Alexander

knew very well that every minute they spent searching put them at greater risk of detection by the French. If that happened, their best hope was to make a run for *Resolution*. Desdemona was swift, and if the French did catch them, Biscuit was quite the fighter. Alexander gave no thought to surrender, for surely that meant being hanged as spies—and who knew what fate for their gryphons.

Desdemona shrieked urgently and pulled to the east, nearer the coast. Amelia gave her gryphon free rein. With a few powerful beats of her wings, the gryphon put on a burst of speed that Biscuit was hard pressed to follow. Alexander held on for dear life as they dropped through a low cloud and leveled out over yet another winter-blasted French field.

"What is it?" he called.

"She smells something."

The farm below was not much. He saw a low-slung stone farmhouse with thatch roof, surrounded by a muddy farmyard and a collection of outbuildings. A couple of milk cows nosed at the brown grass and chickens scratched in the dirt. No humans were in sight.

Captain Amelia signaled Rigley, and the gryphons descended. Desdemona landed gracefully but Biscuit came down with a thump like a lump of dough, so hard that Professor Hobhouse nearly toppled from his saddle. The four of them unbuckled and slipped off their gryphons. Amelia and Rigley drew their swords, and Alexander touched the butt of the pistol in his belt to reassure himself. Only Professor Hobhouse did not draw a weapon.

Their arrival seemed to have gone unnoticed. Not so much as a dog barked. And yet the silence itself seemed threatening.

"It's almost as if they knew someone was coming," Alexander said. "I don't care for this quietude."

"Desdemona smelled something. I know she did. Keep your eyes open."

The four of them spread out and moved as silently as possible toward the barn. The gryphons guarded their backs.

Desdemona lifted her head toward the barn and made soft, birdlike sounds.

"They must be in the barn!"

Without waiting for the others, Alexander ran across the farm yard and threw open the barn door. The day was dark, but the interior was yet darker. He stepped inside and found himself face to face with a large, bearded man wielding a pitchfork.

"Arrêtez!" the man shouted. Alexander guessed from the pitchfork tines just inches from his face that the farmer had just warned him to stop.

Captain Amelia came forward with a raised

pistol, but the Frenchman did not put down the pitchfork. He had a wild look in his eyes.

From inside the barn, a familiar voice called, "It's all right, Pierre. These are friends. Mon amis."

Slowly, the farmer lowered his pitchfork. Amelia did the same with her pistol. Alexander ran deeper into the barn, where he could pick out Lemondrop's glowing yellow eyes in the gloom.

Lord Parkington stood beside the gryphon, holding a pistol in one hand and a sword in the other. Around his head was a bandage stained with blood. Alexander ran up and grabbed his friend by the shoulders and gave him a good shake. "Toby! We found you, all right."

The flyer gave him a broad, genuine smile. But the young lord was more pale than ever and his eyes looked drawn with pain or worry.

"Pierre saw you circling a while ago and sent his family to hide in the woods," Lord Parkington said. "He thought it might be a French patrol looking for me. Then he came in the barn. We heard you land and heard voices, so we were afraid the French had found us out."

Captain Amelia spoke up. "Mr. Parkington, please explain why a Frenchman is hiding you in his barn."

"He has his reasons," Parkington said. "I can tell you about that later."

"Can we trust him?" Amelia asked. She looked

at the French farmer, who still stood gripping his pitchfork.

"He has risked his life for me so far."

"Then the sooner we're gone from here, the better for us all," Amelia said. "The skies are full of gryphons and the roads are full of cuirassiers. We need to get moving. How badly are you hurt?"

Parkington touched the bandage. "One of the French flyers grazed my temple with a pistol ball and knocked me out," he said. "Pierre's wife fixed me up. I'm fine now. It's Lemondrop who's hurt. The French chased him all the way to the coast and he must have gotten into a fight with them. He was raked rather badly. He can't fly."

"Well," said Amelia. "Let us take a look."

The captain stepped forward to lift the blanket that covered Lemondrop's side. That alone was a bad sign, for a gryphon is not a creature to huddle under blankets. Amelia gasped at what she saw.

"Pierre has been helping me take care of him. He made a poultice to draw off any infection. It's what he uses on his horses."

"I fear it is a grievous wound, my lord," Amelia said quietly. "It may be quite some time before Lemondrop can fly again."

"He did it for me, to save me," Parkington said. "The French would have killed me or captured me otherwise."

"Biscuit can carry three back to the ship,"

Amelia said. "He's a great, strong flyer. As long as we don't run into any French patrols, we'll be fine."

"I'm not leaving Lemondrop here," the flyer said with finality. Not for the first time that day, Alexander was amazed by the bond between flyers and their gryphons.

"Mr. Parkington, you do not tell your superior officer what you are or are not going to do," Captain Amelia snapped. "You do it!"

"Different rules now apply," Parkington said in the cold, steely voice that Alexander recognized as a sign that his lordship was not to be trifled with. "We are on French soil."

"I am your captain!"

"And I am Lord Parkington, cousin to his majesty the king," the flyer said haughtily. "Who are you to command me?"

Amelia and Parkington stared at each other. Had it been possible, Alexander was sure smoke and sparks would have poured from their eyes.

Professor Hobhouse stepped forward and cleared his throat as if beginning a class. "If I may," he began. "I'd like to point out that the weather is getting worse, our gryphons are tired, and a return flight to the *Resolution* would be ill advised. I suggest we see how Lemondrop fares tomorrow morning, and make a decision then."

"Very well," Amelia said. "You make a good case, Hobhouse. We shall have to see. We'll post a lookout while the others rest. Mr. Rigley can go first."

"Aye, aye," said Rigley hurriedly.

"If we can make it until nightfall without any cuirassiers showing up, we should be fine—at least until the morning."

CHAPTER 12

Night came early, which was a relief. Darkness meant they were safe from the prying eyes of passing gryphons or cavalry.

In his broken English, the farmer invited the British to his home for dinner, and they all went. With Desdemona and Biscuit in the barn, it was decided that Lemondrop would be safe enough without any of the *Resolutions* guarding him. Gryphons were very protective of their flyers and of their own, and any stranger who chanced upon the barn would be in terrible jeopardy.

The house was very small, really just a one-room cottage with a sleeping loft above. Yet to Alexander it seemed perfect—cozy and warm against the damp winter night, heated by an enormous stone fireplace. Delicious smells came from a large pot simmering on a crane over the fire, and the table was set with wooden bowls and pewter spoons. Though battered and scarred with use, the heavy wooden table was large enough for them all.

"Mon famile," the farmer said proudly, once they were all seated.

One by one, he introduced his wife Estelle, and their daughters: Chloe and Celeste. Chloe was around fourteen and Celeste was six years old, as she proudly informed them. They both kept smiling shyly at Alexander and the older girl, Chloe, even blushed when he said hello to her. Neither girl seemed as taken with Lord Parkington or with Rigley, who was too old for them.

They had worn their cloaks into the house, but now took them off in the warmth of the kitchen. Chloe murmured appreciatively when she noticed Alexander's sea horse cloak pin, the one he had brought from home. Though the pin was purely decorative because Alexander wore a modern pullover sea cloak, he loved the way it gleamed against the rich wool fabric. The sea horse was more heraldic than pretty, portraying a beast known as a hyppocamp—a fierce, rearing stallion with a wild mane, forelegs that ended in webbed claws, and a body tapering down to a powerful mermaid-like tail. The pin was beautifully wrought in silver and the way the firelight danced over it almost made the sea horse seem alive.

"Les hippocampes balade anglais tels?"

Professor Hobhouse and Pierre laughed. Hobhouse replied to her, "Non, jeune dame, Neptune roulé hippocampes. Ils sont bêtes des Dieux. Neptune rode a seahorse. They were beasts of the Gods."

"And it's against regulations to wear such things on a proper uniform," Captain Amelia sniffed.

Estelle served the delicious hot stew, ladling the bowls to overflowing, and Pierre poured them all a glass of apple cider. There were thick slices of bread fresh from the oven with butter.

"Ragoût de lapin," Pierre said, pointing his spoon at the soup.

"Rabbit stew," Professor Hobhouse translated. "It smells heavenly. Bon appetite!"

For several minutes there was very little sound except that of spoons scraping bowls. Then Captain Amelia finally seemed to remember her manners and asked, "So then, monsieur, how is it that you came to help a British flyer?"

She looked at Hobhouse, expecting him to translate her question. But it was Parkington who answered. "Oh, Pierre wasn't always a farmer, you see. As a young man he went to sea." Parkington babbled something in fluent French to Pierre, and the two conversed for a moment.

"I was not aware you knew the lingua franca, Mr. Parkington," Amelia said with raised eyebrows.

"Yes," he said, without further explanation. "Pierre was shipwrecked off the coast of Breton. A squall blew up and his ship ran upon the rocks and it went to pieces. He clung to a piece of wood for hours and would have been lost, but a British frigate happened by and with great risk in such a storm sent out a boat to pick up Pierre. Our nations were not at war then, and he was treated very well. He even learned a little English. Well, a little. Once he made it back home he vowed never to return to sea. He became a farmer. When I appeared yesterday he said it was his time to repay the debt he owed the Royal Navy for saving his life."

"C'est vrai," Pierre said, nodding approvingly.

"It appears, Hobhouse, that we might not have needed you, after all."

"Well, I shall try to make myself useful one way or another," he said.

Captain Amelia raised her glass of cider in the universal gesture that needed no translation. She smiled. "Salut!"

When they had finished eating, Alexander and Rigley insisted on helping the girls and their mother clean up, even though she objected. The flyers were all exhausted—none of them had slept well the night before and the day's tension had sapped all their energy—but it was apparent that the French family wasn't ready to turn in. It had been a long time since they had seen this kind of excitement.

Once the table had been cleared, Pierre poured them all coffee. If that seemed leisurely under the circumstances, it was because they were not so worried about French patrols because a cold, heavy rain was falling. It was the best guard they could have wished for, because no gryphons would be flying in this weather, and the roads were far too dark and wet for cavalry.

They were just about as safe as they could be. And yet an awkward silence fell across the room as their little group realized they might be in for a long evening together. Their two nations were at war, even if there was a truce in the modest farmhouse.

The little French family sat on one side of the table, and the *Resolutions* sat upon the other. Communication was halting at best, with Pierre having his broken English while only Hobhouse and Toby spoke any French. The crackling fire seemed to grow louder in the silence, as did the soft drumming of the rain on the farmhouse roof.

Pierre said a few words to his wife, who seemed to consider what he had said, then nodded in agreement and went to the kitchen. Pierre fetched a bottle and poured each of the adults a glass of rich red wine, giving Rigley a conpiratorial wink as he did so. Estelle returned with a huge earthenware bowl. It was clearly old, the surface glazed with cracks, and yet the bowl was elegant in its simplicity. The farmer's wife said something to one of her daughters, who got up and returned with a pitcher of water that she used to fill the bowl. The water swirled about and then lay still as glass.

Pierre spoke to Lord Parkington, who shrugged, then explained to the rest of them: "Pierre says his wife has some skill in scrying, if we should wish to pass the time."

"Oh," Captain Amelia said. It was a noise of disdain. Scrying was a method that peasants—and gypsies—used to tell fortunes and predict someone's future. A talent for it was often passed down from mother to daughter, though men were occasionally known to have the gift. In England, scrying parties were sometimes held for entertainment—though there were some who put great store in these predictions of the future and regularly sought out those with the ability.

"I think it sounds like a fine idea, and it would only be polite," Lord Parkington said. He said as much to Pierre in French while Captain Amelia scowled at him, but his lordship seemed not to notice.

Lord Parkington went first. There were various methods one practiced in the art could use for scrying with a bowl of water, which served as a looking glass into the future. The person whose future was being read could blow across the bowl, or dip a hand in. Once that was done, some essence of the person was left behind in the water. By staring into the bowl, the person who had the gift of scrying could tell what the future held.

Lord Parkington put his hand into the bowl and took it out when the farmer's wife nodded. She stared intently at the water. The woman suddenly looked up sharply at Lord Parkington and said something in rapid French that made the boy turn red. Professor Hobhouse chuckled.

"Well?" Captain Amelia asked, clearly curious. "If you've made us play the game, Parkington, then I hope you shall tell us what she predicted about you."

"She said I shall live a long life," Lord Parkington replied.

"Bollocks," Amelia said. "That's what any gypsy would say. Well, go ahead and keep it to yourself then. I shall go next."

Chloe emptied the bowl for her mother, and then refilled it with fresh water from the pitcher. Alexander had the sense, from seeing how carefully the girl watched her mother go about scrying, that she was learning the art.

Captain Amelia put her hand into the fresh water.

The farmer's wife was a long time studying the bowl. She screwed up her face in concentration, then finally sighed. When she spoke it was with a wistful smile on her face.

"What is it?" Captain Amelia asked impatiently. "Tell me what you see."

The woman answered in French, and this time Professor Hobhouse translated. "She said you have a hard time with men, and yet you don't realize the one you hold dear is so close. Not here in this room, but close to you in your life in the fleet. You will both come to realize this someday, but it will take time. He is already the love of your life, yet you won't admit it to yourself."

"What poppycock and balderdash," Amelia said. "The love of my life! Ha! This scrying is an amusement that's all well and good for a farmer's wife to be playing at, but I don't put much stock in it."

"There's more," Professor Hobhouse said quietly. "She says your gryphon will die saving you, and when you see this happening, you must let her do so, or all will be lost."

At that, Captain Amelia fell silent and looked deeply troubled. "Not Desdemona?" she finally said. "No, I cannot allow it."

"I'll go next," Rigley offered, breaking the awkward silence following the scry regarding Desdemona. He put his hand into the bowl.

The farmer's wife looked just a moment, and

laughed. She smiled as she delivered her verdict.

"You have a happy-go-lucky soul," Lord Parkington interpreted. "She sees no promotion in your future, but what do you care? You love to fly as a bird loves the air. You'll never have a farthing because you spend it all in port. And why not?"

Rigley laughed. "That's me, all right. I don't like the not having a farthing part, but the rest of it about sums things up. She can tell a thing or two about the future, she can!"

They had all gone except Alexander. "Your turn," Lord Parkington said. "Go on."

Alexander felt strangely reluctant to put his hand into the fresh bowl of water. He knew scrying was silly, just a way to pass the time, but all the same there was something ominous about it. He stuck in his hand, then snatched it out again. The water felt cold as if it had been dipped from a wintry stream instead of poured from the pitcher there in the room.

Pierre's wife looked for a long time. She gripped the sides of the bowl as if forcing herself to stay there, which she had not done before. Then with a cry of dismay she pushed her chair away from the table, snatched up the bowl, and hurled the water into the fire, where it evaporated in a hiss of steam and smoke.

"Aye, and that can't be good," Rigley said.

When she spoke, the French woman's voice

had changed. Her words sounded low and guttural, not like her own voice at all, but as if some force were speaking through her. Her daughter stared, wide-eyed and frightened. When the woman finished speaking, she refused to come back to the table, but stood by the light of the fire.

"What is it?" Alexander asked. Pierre's wife wouldn't look at him.

Lord Parkington hesitated. "Perhaps some things are better left unsaid."

"Mr. Parkington, if you please, the rest of us have been subjected to these pronouncements of gimcrackery at the hands of this self-appointed seer," Captain Amelia said. "You can surely tell us what she predicted."

Again, Parkington hesitated, but went on when Alexander gave him a nod.

"She saw storms, and fire, and terrible battles," he said quietly.

"Hardly much of a prediction considering that there's a war on," Amelia muttered.

Lord Parkington continued: "She says there is great power in you, Alexander. She says you can summon the Old Power like the gods of Earth, Sea, Wind and Fire. But she fears it may rule you yet and turn you to evil. She does not know for certain." He paused. "She says she does not want you in her house or near her children. She fears for them."

Alexander swallowed. "Then I shall take my leave. Please thank her, and tell her I shall be sleeping in the barn."

Rigley reached over the slapped him on the shoulder. He'd had liberal amounts of the rich red French wine. "I reckon it's the barn for you tonight, Alexander. Ha, ha! Don't you worry, it's a good thing for you that gryphons ain't so particular as these Frenchies here."

✻ ✻ ✻

Alexander wasn't yet ready for bed. He was exhausted after rising so early and from the long, tense flight into France. At the same time, his heart was still pumping with the excitement of the mission. They were in France! At any moment they might be overrun and captured by French troops swarming out of the darkness, but Alexander found the thought of thumbing his nose at Napoleon to be more thrilling than frightening.

His nerves singing, he decided to accompany Captain Amelia as she made one last check of the farm before turning in for the night. The darkness was impenetrable beyond the little house, barn, and farmyard. It was raining harder, and they were soon wet through.

"You did well today, Mr. Hope," the flyer

captain said, taking Alexander by surprise. "It's not just anyone who can adapt so well to flying. You show some skill for it. If you should ever decide to switch branches of the service, I should be glad to put in a good word for you."

"Can that be done?"

"It is frowned upon, it's true, but you are just beginning your service, so I'm sure an exception would be made."

"That's very kind of you, but Captain Bellingham sponsored me, and I feel a duty toward him."

"Captain Bellingham is a good man," Amelia agreed. "I know these last few weeks can't have been easy on you, Mr. Hope. You have been thrust into navy life at a rather late age and I've heard the ensigns' mess isn't always ... civil."

"If I'd gone away to a boarding school instead of the navy, I likely would have encountered the same situation," Alexander said sourly.

"I know a bit about what it's like to be an outsider, you know, being that I'm a *her* in *His* Majesty's service. Now, considering that it's improper to say such things about the service and that poaching promising young officers for one's own branch is considered bad form, if you repeat anything of this private conversation I shall have my gryphon peck out your heart."

"Yes, Captain." Alexander was glad the darkness hid his smile, though he thought the flyer commander might be half serious.

Captain Amelia peered into the wet night. "It would be better to post a watch," she said. "We are in enemy territory, after all. But there are only four of us, and we'll need our sleep—and our strength—to get back to the *Resolution*."

"Gryphons have keen ears and a good sense of smell, haven't they? They can alert of us to any trouble," Alexander said as they trudged side by side through the darkness at the edge of the little farm yard. The road was some ways off, screened from the house by an orchard. Fortunately for them, the road was not well traveled.

"Gryphons are better than guard dogs, to be sure," Amelia replied. "But it's not really the French cavalry I'm thinking of tonight. The rain will keep them from patrolling. I'm more concerned that this Frenchie farmer is going to slip out and give us up."

"Pierre? I don't think so, Captain. I feel we can trust him."

Amelia harrumped. "Well, see how you feel when the Napoleonist cavalry shows up. But in any case, I'd say we don't have much choice at the moment. We are certainly not flying out of here tonight, not in this rain. Get some sleep, Mr. Hope. We'll have to hope Pierre doesn't play us all for fools."

He didn't need to be told twice. Captain Amelia and Professor Hobhouse were to sleep in

Pierre's loft, but Alexander and the flyers had been relegated to the barn. But it was dry enough, and he gladly slipped inside, calling out, "It's just me!" as he did so. He really didn't want Rigley skewering him with a pitchfork, thinking he was a cuirassier.

Exhausted, he made his way to the stall where his lordship was leaning up against Lemondrop, reading by the light of a candle. He mumbled a greeting and sat down on a straw bale to pull off his boots, then began to take off his damp uniform. Alexander was tired of his wet clothes and thought there was just enough warmth in the barn that they had some chance of drying before morning.

"I'm getting out of these wet things," Alexander said, tugging off his shirt. "Do you have a spare blanket, by any chance? Mine's packed away."

Parkington nodded and tossed him a blanket. The cool night air felt good on Alexander's bare, clammy skin. He hung his damp uniform off the sides of the stall.

"Tell me something, Toby. What did Pierre's wife say about you tonight?"

"If you must know, Alexander, she said something about me being so full of myself that she was going to need a bigger bowl."

"Ha, ha! I guess she's never tried scrying the future of an English lord before."

Alexander wrapped himself in the blanket, grateful for its dry warmth, and settled into the straw well away from the gryphon. To his horror, his lordship lay down next to the beast.

"Good night," he said.

"Good night," Alexander answered. He was asleep as soon as he closed his eyes.

CHAPTER 13

Sleeping naked, wrapped in a scratchy wool blanket under a pile of straw while a gryphon snored nearby and enemy cavalry prowled the darkness wouldn't have seemed to be much of a recipe for a good night's sleep, but the next time Alexander opened his eyes it was morning.

More of the same weather, he saw: gloomy skies, rain, cold. Vive la France, indeed. It seemed to him nothing more than a sodden, chilly country. He burrowed out from under the straw and tugged the blanket around him against the chill. Toby was already awake and sipping coffee laced with cream from a chipped mug.

Alexander found another battered mug of coffee awaiting him and helped himself. For breakfast, there was a basket of fresh-baked bread and sweet butter. The farmer and his family were being very generous and kind, sharing what little they had. Clearly, Pierre had not slipped away during the night to summon a squadron of cuirassiers, as Captain Amelia had feared.

"How is Lemondrop this morning?" Alexander asked.

"Better, but he still needs his rest." The flyer reached out to stroke the wounded gryphon's nose. Lemondrop's bright yellow eyes fluttered open, then closed again.

"It looks like we won't be doing any flying today," Alexander said. "Not in this dirty weather."

"No matter," Parkington said. "We'll take as long as Lemondrop needs. I'm not leaving her behind."

Alexander didn't want to contradict his friend, but he felt that his lordship might be putting them at great risk—all for the sake of Lemondrop. Captain Amelia had come to rescue Lord Parkington—an earl and cousin of the king, and therefore someone who could become an important pawn or hostage if captured by the Napoleonists. They had not come to rescue a gryphon.

He peered through a crack in the barn wall at the gray mist and drizzle. It really did look like they would be grounded for at least another day.

He checked on his clothes, which weren't quite dry. The thought of abandoning the warm blanket to put on his damp trousers was not all that appealing.

"Are you going to get dressed properly, or are you going to parade about all day like one of those savages from the colonies?"

Before Alexander could answer, Rigley came around for his breakfast. He looked rumpled and unshaven, with bits of straw sticking in his hair. Rigley slurped his coffee and tore at his bread so ravenously that crumbs scattered everywhere. "I do believe that's the latest I've slept in twenty years of service to His Majesty." He raised his mug. "Maybe the French ain't so bad after all."

Parkington gave him a sour look. "You won't be saying that if a squadron of cuirassiers shows up."

Rigley just laughed. "Not much danger of that today unless they come riding in on giant ducks. The Frenchies don't like to get wet any more than we do and that fancy armor they wear gets rusty in the rain. No, it's a good day to rest—and to heal." He nodded at Lemondrop. "We'll get him back in the air yet, my lord, don't you worry."

They had just finished breakfast when Professor Hobhouse and Captain Amelia arrived, leading an old sheep for the gryphons' breakfast. The captain handed the rope to Rigley, who eyed the sheep with skepticism. "Mostly wool and gristle, is that one."

"It's not much, but it will have to feed Biscuit and Desdemona. Lemondrop will be better off with a nice grain mash. Pierre only has so many sheep and we can't have him running around buying up his neighbors' sheep with English silver, now can we?"

"Oh, the gryphons won't complain. They don't much go for coffee and fresh-baked bread, so this old sheep will do them fine."

Professor Hobhouse had borrowed several ingredients from the farmer's wife to make a poultice for Lemondrop's wound. The gryphon growled a warning as he approached, but Lord Parkington soothed him and together they applied the healing poultice.

Captain Amelia looked around the barn and put her hands on her hips. "Right. We'll spend the day in two-hour watches along the road. It's not likely that the enemy will have patrols out, but the Napoleonists have their spies and lookouts, as do we. It's possible that we were seen flying into France and that someone may be searching for us, no matter the weather." She glared at Alexander. "And for Jupiter's sake, Mr. Hope, put on some clothes!"

✷ ✷ ✷

Alexander had the first watch and spent the morning hidden at the base of a huge tree near a bend in the road, where he could see in both directions for a long way.

At first, the swish of wind in the branches and the dripping rain sounded to him like the clatter and jangle of an approaching enemy patrol. Each swirl of mist threatened to reveal a cuirassier. But none appeared, and he might have fallen asleep if he hadn't been so damp and uncomfortable, even wrapped in a heavy oilcloth that still smelled of salt air from the *Resolution*.

He returned to the barn shivering and wet to find Lord Parkington sitting against Lemondrop, gently stroking the gryphon's head. The great beast raised his head weakly to look at Alexander. The yellow eyes looked dull with pain. Alexander was shocked to see that the flyer's own eyes were red and puffy, as if he had been crying.

Parkington swiped at his nose with the back of his hand.

"You must think me a fool," he muttered. "Sniveling over a gryphon."

"Not in the least," Alexander replied. "In fact, there were times when I wondered if you had a heart at all, or if you were carved out of marble like a statue come to life."

"What a horrible thing to say, Alexander!"

"It's just that you're so sure of yourself," Alexander said. "You are so utterly confident. I suppose it's because you are an earl, and you know it. I admire that. Most of the time, I just feel like a boy who's been given a uniform and told to play at being a navy ensign without any real instructions. Only if I mess up, somebody might be killed."

"You're doing fine, Alexander. You are one of the bravest people I know, man or boy, officer or sailor—and *you* don't seem to know it so your head isn't big like it would be with some. You're brave without the bravado. And you have gifts."

Alexander held up his hands and inspected them. "Gifts? Ha! What good are they when I don't even understand how to use them?"

"Give it time, Alexander."

Alexander stood up and pulled a corner of the blanket covering Lemondrop over the other boy's shoulders. "I'll take your watch," he said. "You stay here with Lemondrop."

He grabbed a slice of leftover bread from the basket and his dripping oilcloth, then started toward the door.

"Alexander," Parkington said. "I forgot to add something to your list of talents. You are a good friend."

❀   ❀   ❀

By late afternoon, the rain had let up. Pierre's

daughters, Celeste and Chloe, had been cooped up inside the farmhouse doing endless chores assigned by their mother. They were eager to escape, even if it meant nothing more exciting than running an errand. They met Alexander as he was coming off his watch.

He was wet, tired and hungry—come to think of it, he was always hungry these days—but glad to accept their invitation to come along. Celeste was just a child, but Chloe was close to his own age. She had pretty brown eyes and smiled and laughed a lot. He felt shy and clumsy around her, but Chloe's presence was almost enough to make Alexander forget they were deep in France and in desperate straits.

Alexander spoke only a smattering of French and the girls had only a few words of English, but he understood Chloe's smile and "come with me" wave well enough. He pieced together that they were going to bring their father an afternoon snack at his mill. The girls' mother might be wary of Alexander after what she had seen while scrying, but she must not have warned away her daughters.

In halting English, Chloe explained that it was hard for a farmer who had no sons—or many children, for that matter—to work the farm. So he had built a small mill on the stream that ran through their farm. He ground corn and wheat for their neighbors and made enough to support the family.

They followed a well-worn and very muddy path through the wet fields to the mill. It was a one-story wooden building with a thatched roof built beside a stream about twenty feet across. Beside it churned a waterwheel about ten feet high and two feet wide. Chloe explained that the stream normally flowed slowly, but with the rain the water had risen, and so Pierre thought to make good use of the extra power. As they approached, Celeste ran close to the edge of the swollen stream and Chloe gave her a sharp warning. "Non!"

Inside the mill, Pierre was busy moving sacks of grain. Alexander was surprised to see Rigley helping him.

"Least we can do for the man feeding us is to lend a bit of a hand," Rigley explained. He had taken off his uniform coat to carry grain, throwing the heavy burlap sacks over his shoulder as if they weighed no more than pillows. Like most flyers, Rigley was slightly built, but Alexander could see that he was deceptively strong. "You just coming off watch?"

"Yes. Professor Hobhouse has taken over."

"See anything?"

Alexander shook his head. "Not so much as a passing cart."

"Good," Rigley said, then grunted as he hefted another sack of grain. "If our luck holds for another day or two, maybe we can get Lemondrop back in the air and fly out before them nasty cuirassiers gets word of us."

"Can I help here?"

"No offense, lad, but I reckon these sacks weigh as much as you do." Rigley glanced at the farmer's daughter and smiled. "Besides, I suspect Miss Chloe here wouldn't mind your company on the walk home. She's a bit sweet on you."

Alexander felt his cheeks burn. It amazed him that he had flown on a gryphon into aerial combat, even leaped into a stormy sea without thinking, but Rigley's comment that a girl was sweet on him made Alexander's knees go weak.

The girls left the food with their father, who sat down on the growing pile of grain sacks to share it with Rigley. Back outside, Alexander could see that the mill was set in a small valley. Off to the left was an orchard, and beyond that a field ringed with a stone wall. A few sheep grazed on the grass there.

The churning waterwheel was fascinating to watch. Alexander had never studied one up close. The wheel was ringed by a series of scoops that filled with water from the racing stream, making the shaft through the center of the wheel turn the millstone that ground the grain inside. As the wheel spun round, the scoops were turned upside down and emptied back into the stream, only to be filled again a moment later.

Chloe scolded her little sister, who had gone too close to the raging stream again. The younger girl ran up the bank, skipping and laughing. Chloe saw Alexander watching the waterwheel and came to stand next to him.

"Have you never seen a waterwheel?" she asked.

"Bien sur!" Alexander replied in his own broken French. "But your father built this waterwheel. He must be a very smart man."

"Mon Per c'est magnifique!"

Alexander laughed. Her father was magnificent to have built this himself. At the same time, he felt a pang. How was it that people like Pierre and Chloe were supposed to be his enemy? Of course, Pierre had experienced English decency himself after being rescued at sea and so had a different viewpoint than most of his countrymen, who only believed what they were told about the English.

He had to remind himself that Pierre and Chloe were not French soldiers. They were not Napoleon, who as a dictator and conqueror ruled people as he saw fit, ignoring the natural rights any Englishman possessed—or any human being, for that matter.

A scream interrupted his thoughts. To his horror, he saw that little Celeste had fallen into the flooded stream and was clinging desperately to some brush overhanging the water.

"Celeste!" her sister cried. She and Alexander ran to pull her out.

But the current was too strong. They were too far away to reach Celeste in time. Celeste lost her grip and was swept into the center of the stream, beyond their reach. In seconds, she would be carried into the waterwheel and crushed.

Now Chloe was screaming as she looked on helplessly. *What can I do?* Alexander raised his hand and willed the water to stop. Nothing happened. He closed his eyes and tried to focus on the water in his mind's eye. He shouted at it silently. *Stop!* He opened his eyes. Nothing. Celeste was as good as dead.

And then a miracle. Pierre burst from the mill house with a length of rope into which he had tied a loop at the end. His first throw went right to Celeste. She caught it and held on tight. Pierre waded as far out into the stream as he dared, with Rigley closer to the bank, holding on to Pierre's belt at the back.

Slowly, shouting encouragement to her, Pierre pulled his daughter closer. Finally, he had her in his arms. Then Pierre slipped, and they were both pulled under. Chloe screamed in utter despair. But Rigley was still hanging on to Pierre. His face contorted with effort as he used one powerful arm to swing them closer to the bank while grabbing hold of a tree root with the other hand.

Pierre must have managed to get his feet back

under him, because he reappeared, gasping for breath, with Celeste still in his arms. With Rigley's help, they managed to get into shallow water. Then all three got out of the stream and collapsed on the safety of the bank. Chloe ran to them.

Alexander's heart was pounding. Celeste and Pierre had very nearly died. He had been utterly unable to do anything about it. He had thought he would use whatever power he imagined he might have to save Chloe's little sister. And yet it was Pierre who had rescued her—using a length of rope. He felt completely useless.

Watching Pierre hug his two girls on the stream bank, he also felt an enormous sense of relief. Another second or two, and events would have had a very different ending.

Right then and there, Alexander vowed not to rely on his power again—if he even had any actual power. Better to trust to quick action and a sturdy length of rope than some silly power!

❈ ❈ ❈

The next day they awoke to golden sunshine. Lemondrop seemed stronger after breakfast, though he went right back to sleep. It appeared they would have to hide out at the farm for at least one more day, though each hour they spent in France heightened the danger that they would be discovered and captured.

Alexander helped feed and water the other gryphons and then stood his watch along the country road. As the shadows lengthened toward afternoon, there was still no sign of any French patrols. He returned to the barn, where he found Chloe and Celeste waiting for him. The girls were all smiles and he greeted them in his broken French.

"What do they want?" Captain Amelia asked him.

"I take it that they want me to go exploring with them."

"Exploring?" The flyer captain glanced from Alexander to Chloe's apple-cheeked face and seemed to grow flustered. "Oh. I see. Well, I don't suppose there's any harm in it if you don't stray too far."

Alexander turned to Lord Parkington. "Toby, won't you come with us?"

"I should stay here with Lemondrop."

The young lord still sat with his back against the gryphon. Neither of them appeared to have moved for hours. Lord Parkington, who was already so pale, his head still bandaged, now looked lethargic and sickly in the dappled sunshine that filtered into the barn.

Much to Alexander's surprise, Captain Amelia spoke up and ordered Lord Parkington to accompany him. "There's nothing more you can do here while Lemondrop is sleeping," she said. "Go with Mr. Hope. Perhaps you can keep him out of trouble."

She added this last statement with a sniff. As Lord Parkington shrugged into his coat, Desdemona came over and nuzzled against Lemondrop, and then settled in next to him. Not for the first time, Alexander was surprised by how gracefully the gryphons moved. Desdemona curled herself up as quietly as a kitten, though she was many times larger—more lion than barn cat.

They left the barn and Chloe led the way toward the orchard. Much to Alexander's relief, Chloe didn't seem to blame him for not being the one to save Celeste. Of course, she hadn't known he was even trying. Alexander still felt foolish for attempting to summon a power he wasn't really even sure he had. The sheer terror they had lived through yesterday, watching Celeste nearly drown, made them glad to be alive.

Though it was winter, the afternoon air felt sun-kissed and warm. In the orchard, although the branches were bare, there was a lingering scent of apples and peaches. A few stray apples still lay among the leaves and they startled a deer that had been dining on these windfalls. Orchards were like old friends to Alexander, who had raided his share back home. He found a few choice apples that the frost and deer had missed, then shared them with the others.

They flopped on the ground with their backs against the fruit trees and dined on the apples, which were all the sweeter now that their flavor had been concentrated by the winter cold. Alexander ate juicy apple after apple, flinging the cores away among the trees.

"You seem right at home, Alexander," said Lord Parkington, munching an apple.

"Of course I am," he replied. "If we didn't need to keep one eye open for the enemy, I believe I would take a nap."

Celeste jumped up, a mischievous grin on her face. She walked over to Alexander and thumped him on the shoulder, then ran away laughing. Chloe ran off as well, giggling riotously.

"What in the world?" Lord Parkington asked.

"Haven't you ever played tag?" Alexander cried as he jumped up. "Run!"

He ran after the girls, who dodged between the tree trunks. He almost caught Celeste, but then pretended to trip so that she could get away, leaving a trail of delighted squeals in her wake. Chloe was extremely hard to catch. She seemed to be as swift as the deer they had come across earlier.

"She's faster than you are, Alexander!" Toby called. "You'll never catch her!"

He wasn't about to give up. With a final burst

of speed, he leaped around an apple tree and tagged her. Chloe laughed with delight and Alexander felt his heart glow in a way it never had before. Then she raced off after her sister.

Warmed by the exercise, the boys took off their uniform coats. They kept up the game among the trees for nearly half an hour until all four of them finally sprawled on the orchard floor, breathless and red-faced. Alexander found it hard to catch his breath because he was laughing so hard. It had been a long time since he had played a game and had so much fun.

He collapsed onto his back and watched the winter sun through the web of branches overhead. Someone took his hand and he looked over to see Chloe smiling at him from where she lay on a blanket of apple leaves. Alexander's heart, still hammering in his chest, seemed to skip a beat. With luck, he thought, they would be able to spend a few more days at the farm.

By now the late afternoon sun was waning and they decided to start back to the house and barn. They stood and gathered up their coats, then stuffed a few of the less worm-eaten apples into their pockets for the gryphons.

Celeste saw them first. She gasped, and the others looked up to see where she was pointing.

Cavalry. Riding for the orchard.

They ran.

CHAPTER 14

"We must warn the others!" Lord Parkington cried. He jabbered something in French to Chloe, who suddenly sprinted ahead.

"Where's she going?"

"She's a much faster runner than we are," Parkington explained. "We'll only slow her down. We've been at sea so long that our legs haven't got the feel of land anymore."

"Speak for yourself," Alexander said, but as he watched Chloe rapidly increasing the distance between them, he had to agree. Chloe was their best chance of outrunning the French cavalry. Alexander reached for Celeste's hand to help the small girl along and they ran faster.

"How did they find us?" he panted.

"It was only a matter of time," Toby responded. "I had hoped we would have a few more days, but someone must have seen us and gone to the local officials. Maybe one of the farmers on the way to Pierre's mill spotted us."

He was surprised to see that the French were not rushing headlong toward the barn. Several horsemen spread out, creating a perimeter around the field beyond the orchard. Another horseman settled in beside Pierre's mill. "They're setting up a circle around the farm. They mean to trap us!"

Alexander studied the French riders. These cuirassiers wore uniforms very similar to French flyers. Their coats were blue with red-fringed epaulets, with white breeches and knee-high black boots. They wore steel breastplates, polished to a mirror finish that flashed in the winter sun.

He wasn't sure if this partial armor would stop a musket ball, but it certainly looked impressive. The French also wore steel helmets with black horsehair crests that added several inches in height to all the riders, making them look like giants in the saddle. Finally, they all carried pistols and heavy cavalry sabers that jangled menacingly in their scabbards as the horses trotted into position.

There must have been at least twenty cuirassiers spread about the field, and who knew how many positioned where they couldn't be seen.

"This doesn't look good," Alexander managed to pant.

"Save your breath and run!"

They sprinted the final distance into the farmyard, scattering chickens and geese that squawked in protest. Alexander pointed Celeste toward the farmhouse, where her mother stood in the doorway, calling to her daughter.

Chloe had beat them to the barn and given the warning that the farm was surrounded. She stood off to one side looking worried, her father's arm around her shoulders. Alexander suddenly realized there could be terrible consequences for this family. The cuirassiers would not take kindly to the fact that they had harbored British refugees.

Captain Amelia was busy barking orders at Rigley and Professor Hobhouse. They were getting the flying saddles onto Biscuit and Desdemona, but both gryphons were skittish in the excitement, stepping this way and that as the flyer and schoolmaster tried to buckle the straps into place.

"Professor Hobhouse was on watch and he reports that the French are massed along the road in front of the farm, probably waiting for the riders you saw in the fields to get into position," Amelia explained.

"How many?" Alexander asked.

"Maybe fifty altogether, from the sounds of it. Far too many for us to take on. The only way out is up. Apparently the horsemen have no scout gryphons with them, Jupiter be praised."

"What about Pierre and his family?" Alexander asked. "They're in awful danger now. Can't they come with us?"

"I have a contingency plan for that," Amelia said. She gestured for Pierre to come closer so that she could explain. "Pierre will tell the cuirassiers that we held his daughters hostage to ensure his cooperation."

"Such lies!" Lord Parkington protested. "We're English, not monsters!"

"Lies will keep Pierre and his family safe. The French will be only too glad to assume we've acted in such a barbaric manner."

"But we would never—"

"There are times when one must have broad shoulders, my Lord Parkington," the captain said, addressing him by his formal title. "It would be much too dangerous for this good family to be seen as cooperating with us. Mr. Rigley? Do it now, if you please."

"Aye, aye, Captain." Rigley sighed, stepped up to Pierre, and punched him hard in the eye and then in the mouth. Chloe gave a frightened cry. Rigley stepped back to admire his work, then patted Pierre gently on the shoulder. "You'll have a nice shiner and a fat lip, mon frere. Very convincing. Now if I were you, I'd get down to the house before the shooting starts. That farmhouse of yours has thick stone walls that are going to come in handy when the bullets start flying."

Pierre nodded and smiled grimly, then spat a stream of blood onto the packed earth of the barn floor. He took Chloe's hand and led her out of the barn. The girl looked back once at Alexander, who gave her a small smile. He realized as he did so that he would never see her again. As she turned to go, Alexander called out her name.

"Chloe!"

Startled, the girl stopped in the doorway. Alexander ran over and gave her his cloak pin, the one shaped like a sea horse, that she had so admired. The girl's face lit up.

"For the friendship you have shown us, Chloe."

The girl took the cloak pin and gave him the briefest of kisses, her lips just brushing his cheek. Alexander felt his face burn red.

"Mr. Hope, we haven't got all day!" Captain Amelia barked.

"Sorry, Captain," Alexander managed to stammer. He looked back over his shoulder to see Chloe and her father hurrying toward the farmhouse.

"We're moving out right now before the bloody French get a chance to charge us," Captain Amelia said. "Mr. Hope, you're with me again on Desdemona. Professor Hobhouse, and Mr. Parkington, you're with Mr. Rigley on Biscuit. Saddle up, gentlemen, and be quick about it."

Lord Parkington spoke up. "I'm not on Biscuit! I'll be flying Lemondrop."

Looking at Parkington, Captain Amelia said, "Mr. Rigley, give me your pistol."

Rigley gave the captain a loaded pistol, and she strode toward Lemondrop. Lord Parkington hurried to put himself between the captain and the wounded gryphon. "No, you can't!" Parkington cried.

"We must do what is necessary," Captain Amelia said, an uncharacteristic note of gentleness in her voice. "Lemondrop still can't fly. Would you prefer that he fall into Napoleonist hands? If he takes to the air again they'll make him carry a French flyer to attack our own ships. Or they'll make him into a breeder and clip his wings so he can't fly off. Either way, Lemondrop won't like it, so they'll be cruel in forcing him to obey. Is that the life you would choose for your gryphon? Wouldn't a pistol shot be better?"

Captain Amelia cocked the pistol and put it against Lemondrop's head. Alexander turned away. He understood that a horse with a broken leg must be shot, but somehow gryphons seemed more than a horse. He suspected that Captain Amelia was right, but he didn't want to watch Lemondrop's life being ended.

"Lemondrop! Get up!" Lord Parkington's voice was anguished. "I suppose you would have shot *me* if I couldn't fly."

"Please stop making this so difficult," the captain said. "Now get back and let me do what I must."

But the gryphon lurched to his feet, forcing Captain Amelia to take a step back. If another second had passed, it might have been too late. Lemondrop shook himself and looked around as if seeing his surroundings for the first time. Only this morning his eyes had appeared dull and listless, but now they seemed to glow with a piercing yellow light as Lemondrop looked around the barn. Then the gryphon unfurled his massive wings and gave a kind of yawn.

"You see, I told you he could fly!" Parkington ran to get Lemondrop's saddle.

But there was no time. Outside, they heard someone shouting orders in French and the jangle of cavalry harness. Alexander pressed an eye to a crack in the barn wall. There were now half a dozen French troopers in the farmyard, facing the barn. "We're surrounded!" he hissed.

"Nelson's hat!" Captain Amelia uncocked the pistol and handed it to Rigley. "There's nothing to be done now but make a run for it. Mr. Rigley, get on your gryphon. I want you and Biscuit to rush them as soon as the door opens. Mr. Hope, get that barn door open and then get aboard Desdemona quick as lightning. Lemondrop and Mr. Parkington will follow behind us as best they can. Got your pistols ready, Professor?"

"Indeed."

"Now!"

Alexander ran for the barn entrance. They had barred the double doors after Pierre and Chloe left, so he threw off the length of timber and shoved the doors wide. He found himself just a few feet from a French cuirassier, so close that he could see the Frenchman's greenish eyes and the shiny buckle on his chin strap.

It was hard to say who was more startled. The cavalryman started to draw his huge saber, then thought better of it and reached for a big pistol in a saddle scabbard. Alexander turned to flee and discovered Biscuit's massive bulk hurtling toward him with Rigley in the saddle, waving a saber and shouting like a madman. He knew that a gryphon springs like a cat with its powerful back legs to help launch itself into the air—but he had never been in *front* of one before.

Alexander dodged out of the way just in time to feel the rush of Biscuit's wings as the gryphon burst out the barn door at the French cuirassiers.

There was a clash of swords. A pistol cracked,

and then another. Something sang past Alexander's ear like a hot and angry bumblebee. He rolled to his feet and ran toward Desdemona. Captain Amelia didn't seem to notice him as he swung aboard. She had both hands on the reins, her eyes straight ahead.

Biscuit had gone out the door like a cannonball, scattering the enemy troops. Now Desdemona leapt after him. But she did not launch herself into the air. She pounced on the nearest cuirassier, slashing at him with her talons, and he toppled from his saddle as his horse bucked in fear. While Desdemona was small for a gryphon—built more for speed to swiftly carry messages and scout enemy movements—no horse was interested in standing up to her.

Quick as a cat, Desdemona spun to confront the next cuirassier and crossed the distance between them in two rapid bounds. The Frenchman was ready for them. Though his horse reared, this man kept his seat and slashed at them with his saber.

A French cavalry saber is wickedly sharp, long and heavy, with a curved blade. Hours of practice drills with that weapon gave a cuirassier muscles like steel, so that his arm was like part of the sword. Cuirassiers were all big men on big horses —the shock troops of the Napoleonist forces. Captain Amelia parried his blade but her own sword was shorter and lighter. He knocked it aside and drove his huge saber at Amelia.

In that instant, Alexander raised his pistol and fired at point blank range. His target disappeared in a burst of smoke. When it cleared a moment later, he saw that the Frenchman lay sprawled in the mud.

More pistols popped around them. Alexander looked up to see a handful of cuirassiers charging them with sabers leveled like lances. The *Resolutions* had lost the element of surprise and were now outnumbered. It was time to flee, not fight. Lucky for them, the French still didn't seem to have any gryphons. Once they were in the air, they would be beyond the reach of the cuirassiers and had a chance of escaping back to the *Resolution*.

What about Lord Parkington on Lemondrop? Alexander looked around the farmyard, expecting to see them. Where were they?

Then he looked back at the barn and his heart sank. Lord Parkington was still on foot, leading Lemondrop by the halter. The gryphon was limping badly and his wings drooped. Alexander hated to admit it, but he wondered if maybe Captain Amelia had been right. Horrible as it seemed, perhaps a bullet was a better alternative for Lemondrop than being captured by the Napoleonists.

"Toby!" he cried. "You have to leave him! There is no time!"

He felt Desdemona shift beneath him as she turned to meet the charging horsemen. In a moment, they would all be overwhelmed and captured because Lemondrop hadn't taken to the air after all.

Then a dark shadow fell out of the sky like a meteor. It was Biscuit, sweeping low over the ground to come at the French horsemen head on. With a piercing war cry, Biscuit caught a rider in his talons and swept another from the saddle with a mighty beat of his wings. From the stern rider's saddle, Professor Hobhouse peppered the French with pistol shots.

The force of the enemy's charge was broken. Biscuit spun as if on a pivot and came at them again from above. Alexander felt a sickening rush in his stomach as Desdemona sprang forward and joined the fight, covering the distance to the French with two quick beats of her wings. His pistols empty, Alexander drew his cutlass and hacked at the French as best he could.

But fighting on the ground from the back of a gryphon was very different from fighting in the air. All the action was up front, and Alexander mostly found himself forced to cling to the saddle as Desdemona balanced on her hind legs to swat and slash at the enemy.

Alexander risked a glance over his shoulder just in time to see Lord Parkington slip onto Lemondrop's back. He hadn't had time to put on the flying harness. It was terribly dangerous to take to the air without a proper saddle and harness. One slip meant falling to your death.

More French were coming from around the back of the barn. "Look out!" Alexander shouted a warning to Lord Parkington.

If Lemondrop could not yet fly, he could run. Favoring his injured side, he dashed ahead of the French attackers. But a gryphon was intended to fly, not gallop fast as a horse, and Lemondrop was injured. The French riders would soon overtake him. The farmhouse and a hedge loomed beyond. Even if Lemondrop could by some miracle outrun the French horses, he was going to run out of room.

Alexander saw Lord Parkington crouch low over Lemondrop's neck and then grip the gryphon's sides firmly with his knees. With the horses right behind him, Lemondrop gave a final burst of speed and launched himself skyward.

"Use your wings!" he heard Lord Parkington shouting. "Lemondrop, there's nothing wrong with your wings!"

The gryphon seemed to hover there for a second, all dead weight hung upon by gravity, and Alexander thought they would crash down again. Then Lemondrop's great wings snapped open and caught the wind. His wings beat the air once, twice, three times—each beat growing stronger and more powerful. The French pursuers were left behind, though one or two snapped off pistol shots at the gryphon. Alexander saw that the French who had been hiding in the woods and orchard were now racing toward the skirmish. More pistol shots came from that direction. A bullet struck a plow in the farmyard and ricocheted with a hair-raising whine.

"Altitude, Mr. Parkington! You must climb!" Captain Amelia shouted. Desdemona seemed to leap straight up as two horsemen came after her at once. Her own wings spread and beat the air. They rose above the heads of the Frenchmen, whose sabers sliced the air where Desdemona had been only a moment before.

They might have swept down and attacked the horsemen, but their goal now was flight, not fight. Desdemona circled higher and the frustrated horsemen cursed at them in French. Below them, Lemondrop was still struggling. His hind legs just grazed the helmets of the French riders—not nearly high enough to clear the hedge at the edge of the farmyard beyond the stone house. Watching, Alexander braced himself for the crash that was just seconds away.

Then he saw Lord Parkington haul on the reins and Lemondrop suddenly swerved up, up, up at the last instant. The hedge behind them, there was nothing ahead but blue sky. Captain Amelia had Desdemona fly in close.

"That's it, Mr. Parkington!" she shouted. "How

does Lemondrop fare?"

"We shall make the coast, at least," came the reply.

"Excellent!"

The wind seemed to snatch away this last word as Captain Amelia urged Desdemona higher. The Napoleonists had a few rifles between them, and with the rifles' greater range a few shots tried to pluck the gryphons from the sky. Unharmed, they were soon out of range of the enemy's guns.

Biscuit fell in to one side so that they had a loose formation. Part of a stern rider's duty was to scan the skies for the enemy, but thankfully Alexander did not see the air interrupted by anything but a few wisps of cloud.

The winter day was already growing short and the sun was past its zenith. Even without enemy gryphons, they faced a great risk that they would not reach the *Resolution* before nightfall. The ship would be sailing a pattern back and forth awaiting their return, but it was no small feat to find a single ship on the English Channel, even when they knew about where to look.

Locating the ship would be impossible at night. They would be in real trouble if darkness caught them over the open water. Gryphons burdened with two riders—let alone slowed down by the wounded Lemondrop—could not possibly make it all the way to England. Exhausted, the gryphons would eventually drop into the frigid waters of the channel.

Alexander fumbled for the speaking tube—it was impossible to shout loud enough for Captain Amelia to hear him over the rushing wind. "Will we make it?" he asked.

"Desdemona is a strong flyer but we may have to lighten our load, Mr. Hope," the flyer captain replied. "I shall begin by jettisoning ensigns who ask annoying questions."

"Aye, aye, Captain."

With the westering sun at their backs, they flew toward the coast. Alexander kept glancing to his left at Lemondrop, who was clearly laboring heavily and slowing them down. With every effort of his wings he seemed to be trying to lift a heavy load. Alexander felt exhausted just watching the gryphon fly.

The wind picked up as they neared the coast—he could see the white blur of surf and the vast blue of the empty sea beyond—and glancing over at Lemondrop and Lord Parkington he felt a fresh wave of worry in his stomach as if he were trying to digest a stone. A saddle and flying harness helped steady a flyer in a strong wind, and Lord Parkington had neither. Bareback on a horse was challenging enough, when a hard fall to the ground was only a few feet away. Bareback on a gryphon, the wind tugged at you constantly, and if you slipped the ground was a long, long way down. Lord Parkington was a strong flyer but it seemed like madness to even attempt such a long flight without a proper saddle.

Alexander glanced to his right and took some reassurance from the big figure of Biscuit lumping along with Rigley at the reins and Professor Hobhouse wearing a silly floppy hat and goggles, all the while scanning the skies. Hobhouse was undeniably scholarly, yet he had a surprising skill with sword and pistol. Alexander would have bet his Sunday dinner that Hobhouse hadn't always had his nose buried in a book.

What he couldn't see was the death grip the professor had on the saddle pommel. *I wouldn't have thought myself so timid in the air,* Hobhouse observed to himself, not for the first time. *These flyers take to the skies daily without a thought, so it is perfectly safe. Yet if I should be so lucky to feel the ground under my feet again or the deck of a ship it would take a direct order from the king himself to get me airborne again.* He gulped, blinked against the sunlight gleaming off Rigley's helmet, and tried to ignore his hammering heart.

Then they were out over the ocean. Lemondrop sank a little lower as he struggled in the stronger wind over the sea and they flew down with him in formation. The waves loomed that much closer, cold and hungry.

Captain Amelia had a flyer's chronometer strapped to her wrist that also functioned as a compass—it was an incredibly expensive device, but she was a flyer captain, after all. The only other flyer that he had seen wearing one was Lord Parkington. It was an extravagant item for an ensign, but what else did one expect from an ensign who also happened to be a lord? Amelia consulted her compass and nudged Desdemona with her knees. Alexander felt the weak winter sun shift somewhat from the back of his neck to his cheek as they adjusted their course.

Alexander's thoughts wandered. He hoped that Chloe and her family would be all right—things would go badly for them if the cuirassiers did not believe their story of being held hostage by the "brutal" English. It was odd to think of her as French—she had seemed so sweet and kind.

There had been nothing so gentle about the cuirassiers. The skirmish in the farmyard had been a close thing, and he wasn't in any hurry to meet a French trooper again.

"Pay attention if you please, Mr. Hope." Captain Amelia's voice, made tinny by the speaking tube, startled him out of his thoughts.

He scanned the skies, and saw three distant specks. His heart hammered. Could those be birds? No ... they were too large at that distance. "French gryphons!"

"I wondered when you might notice them," Amelia said. "They are very far behind us, but they are somewhat swifter." Even with two riders, Desdemona was a very fast gryphon in the air. Amelia didn't have to add that it was Lemondrop slowing them down.

"Will they catch us?"

"That is the question, isn't it, Mr. Hope? Better load your pistols, if you haven't already."

Alexander did just that, and slipped the two heavy flying pistols into their holsters on either side of the saddle. He glanced over at Lemondrop, who was laboring mightily. The pursuit had all the cold logic of Professor Hobhouse's math problems. They were flying at X speed while the French were coming on at Y speed. Over the estimated distance, how long until the enemy overtook them? Alexander feared it was only a matter of a half hour at most.

He looked ahead. The sea spread out before them, glittering with the red and gold of the setting sun. If the Napoleonists didn't catch them, darkness would.

And then a beautiful sight. A white speck on the channel that might have been a trick of the eyes became the *Resolution* with her full sails spread. She looked like some sea bird riding the waves, graceful and alone. Alexander thought it was the best sight he had ever seen.

The French gryphons had been gaining on them but now peeled away, keeping their distance, not wanting to tangle with a British frigate shotted with chain and with a complement of fresh gryphons at the ready.

"A fine sight indeed!" Captain Amelia called through the speaking tube, and then they began a delicious lazy spiral down toward the waiting ship.

CHAPTER 15

The *Resolutions* greeted them like heroes. A great cheer of "Huzzah! Huzzah!" filled the air, and the crew rushed forward to meet them, eager to clap them on the back as if to see if they were real. The usual order and discipline on the ship was quite forgotten as sailors called out questions. Everyone wanted to hear how they had managed to slip away from France, rescuing Lord Parkington and Lemondrop.

Rigley did most of the talking for them, basking in the attention, which was fine by Alexander. Captain Amelia stood off to one side, stroking Desdemona's head and trying to appear aloof from the excitement, though she was clearly listening to Rigley's account with interest and pride.

Alexander stumbled as a huge hand thumped him on the back. He looked up to see Jameson grinning down at him, the big sailor's face hovering over him large as a platter. "Ha, ha, you showed them Frenchies!" he said. "I had me doubts that you'd be much in the way of a true blue sailor when I first seen you, lad, green-faced like you was in that rowboat back in Spithead Harbor. But to fly into France and out again—I never heard the like, ha, ha!"

There were more comments like that. Their exploits had done the men good. It was hard duty aboard a ship in the English Channel in winter, caught between the cold and the constant threat of a Napoleonist attack. The *Resolution* had been cruising back and forth off the French coast, awaiting their return. Each day threatened danger from the skies and seas—an assault in force from a French gryphon squadron or the sudden appearance of enemy sails on the horizon. Now, at long last, the waiting and the tension were over.

The crowd only began to break up when Lord Parkington led Lemondrop away to the gryphon deck. The gryphon limped badly and his wings drooped after the exhausting flight. But the valuable gryphon had returned to the safety of the *Resolution*, where he could regain his full fighting strength.

Captain Bellingham's arrival scattered the rest of the men to their stations. "Well done, well done indeed!" He greeted Captain Amelia with a look of relief and said in a quiet voice: "Amelia, my dear, you have returned. I must admit I had some fears for your safety."

"You would not be rid of me so easily, Bellingham," she said, turning a shade of pink. It wasn't every day that someone called her my dear with so much feeling. She patted Desdemona, who purred like a house cat—a massively overgrown one with claws the size of daggers. "Desdemona and I wouldn't let a few Napoleonists deter us."

They were interrupted by the shrill shouts of the bosun ordering the hands back to work. For the first time, Alexander noticed the activity on deck, which went far beyond the usual running of the ship. Lines were being coiled, stores shifted, and men streamed into the rigging as Lieutenant Swann shouted, "Make sail!"

"What's afoot?" Captain Amelia asked.

"You are just in time." Bellingham smiled broadly. "We were awaiting your return somewhat anxiously for more than one reason. A messenger gryphon came during the night and I have new orders. We are sailing to Gibraltar!"

❈ ❈ ❈

Alexander was dismissed to go below for a much-needed hour of rest. He was still new enough to the routine of the *Resolution* that he wouldn't be much use getting the ship ready for its voyage. Now that they had reached the *Resolution*, he realized how exhausted he was—and yet sleep would be difficult, for he felt the excitement in the air about the voyage ahead.

Ever since they had left Spithead, the ship had been on channel duty, on guard against the French. While Alexander never doubted for a moment that their mission was important and the winter storms on the channel were fierce, it seemed like dull duty compared to the adventure of sailing to Gibraltar, the British-occupied lump of rock at the entrance to the Mediterranean Sea. For a start, it also promised to be much warmer there.

He met Roger on the ladder as he was going down and his friend was coming up.

"You've made it!" Roger cried. "I came running as soon as I heard. We weren't sure where you were because you were due back yesterday and the captain was in a fit to have us bound for Gibraltar. He had the crew jumping about like long-tailed cats in a ship full of rocking chairs."

"Lemondrop was wounded and couldn't fly," Alexander explained. "It took him an extra day and he barely made it as it was."

"Then he got in the air not a moment too

soon." Roger grinned. "Gibraltar! Can you believe it! It's supposed to be semi-tropical. Can you imagine such a thing! Well, I'm on duty again in a moment but you must tell me all about it later."

Roger clapped him on the back, and then scurried up the ladder. Alexander climbed down into the gloom below decks. His nose was accosted by the familiar smells of the ship—damp wood, sea salt, fresh-baked bread from the ship's ovens. He had nearly forgotten those smells, and in remembering that he had forgotten them he felt a pang at how much he had missed them. Only now did he realize how much danger they had faced in flying into France. Yet the danger had been worth it because they had rescued Lord Parkington and Lemondrop—and he had met Chloe.

He passed through the gun deck to the ensigns' quarters at one end and entered the narrow doorway. Sitting at the table in the cramped mess room was Fowler. He had his dagger out and was spinning it point down on the table like a long, sharp top, ignoring the fact that he was gouging a hole in the surface. Alexander froze as Fowler looked up.

"Hello, Hopeless. That's quite a hero's welcome you received. Pity they've wasted it on the likes of you."

Alexander felt a flash of anger run through him like a hot wire. "What do you mean?"

"You think you have us all fooled, don't you? Captain Bellingham and all the rest think you're a hero, but deep down you know the truth, which is that you're a coward."

"How dare you!" The protest sounded weak to his own ears, because it was true that he felt like an impostor who wasn't worthy of the attention he had received. He would have liked to lash out and strike Fowler, but the older boy was much bigger and technically he outranked Alexander. Striking a superior was forbidden in the navy.

"Come now, snotty, don't play the offended little gentleman with me," Fowler said, still twirling the big knife menacingly. "You've got a secret you're hiding from the rest of us. I can tell, because there's something about you. Something I can't quite put my finger on, but I will. There's been talk among the men that you're some sort of elemental. I've got my eye on you, Hopeless. I'm going to ferret out the truth."

Alexander walked past him to his hammock, feeling Fowler's eyes boring into him all the while, sharp as the dagger he toyed with. He pulled his sea chest from under the hammock and opened the lid. There was no lock on anything aboard the *Resolution*, save for the grog room and the armory that held the pistols and swords. Alexander had brought precious little from home, except for the clothes on his back and the silver cloak pin he had given to Chloe.

Inside the chest was a leather-bound book—a history of the defeat of the armada that he had borrowed somewhat permanently from his uncle's library at Kingston Hall, without his uncle's knowing.

In the very bottom of the chest was a spare shirt, and wrapped in that was the wristling that had once been his father's. He took it out now and held it up, amazed at how the sliver glittered in the dim light as if the surface was flecked with tiny stars. Then he wrapped it up and closed the chest.

The excitement of their escape from the enemy was over, so that now waves of exhaustion washed over him. Gratefully, Alexander climbed into his hammock and slept.

❁ ❁ ❁

When Alexander woke, he sensed immediately that something was different about the ship. He heard the sea rushing past the wooden hull just beyond his head—the current had changed, or their direction. He ate a quick breakfast of biscuits and butter with hot coffee mixed with cream and sugar, then went up on deck.

The winter sunshine was brilliant, though the low, slanting sun defined all it touched in sharp contrasts, as if the edges of everything were cut by a knife. To his surprise, he found that he had slept the night through and no one had awakened him for his watch—captain's orders, as it turned out.

"The Irish coast, lad," said Jameson, who was busy shifting barrels so that they could be lashed tight against the gunwales. Beyond him could be seen a rocky coast and hills that looked deeply green, even in winter. "Nothing in Ireland but banshees, wicked red-haired lassies and potatoes, though the whiskey is tolerable good."

Liam was standing nearby, and he snapped out in his distinctly Irish accent, "Belay that talk, Jameson, and see to your work, why don't you?"

The huge sailor only chuckled. "Aye, aye, young sir." The other men worked in pairs to lift the heavy barrels, but Jameson picked one up as if it weighed no more than a baby and set it in place.

Alexander turned to Liam. "Ireland?"

"We're passing the coast where your famous ancestor Sir Algernon Hope wrecked the armada with a storm two hundred years ago," Liam said. "He saved England almost single-handedly, though I don't have to tell *you* that, of all people. Without him we'd all be speaking Spanish, I suppose. The survivors who made it to shore—those who weren't clubbed to death by Irish thieves or eaten by wolves—settled down and that's why they have what we call the Black Irish today. Those are the ones who have black eyes and black hair on account of their Spanish blood."

"Like you, you mean."

"There are rumors about that on my mother's side," Liam said, his coal-black eyes flashing good naturedly. "My father's family is descended from the Normans who conquered England and Ireland." It was no secret that Liam's grandfather was the Earl of Kildare—an old and distinguished Irish family, indeed, though they were not close family to the king as Lord Parkington was, and it was Liam's cousin who would be the next earl. What Liam said next surprised Alexander, as did his bitter tone. "Before the Normans came along, my ancestors were kings. They ruled the whole of Ireland. If it weren't for the English and bloody King George running things, my family might be kings of Ireland again. Ireland would be a free country, and not under the English boot heel."

Alexander was surprised to hear Liam sound so angry toward the English. What was he doing in the Royal Navy if he hated the English so much? Liam moved off to make sure the men lashed down the barrels properly, and Alexander decided that a discussion of Irish rebellion wasn't a conversation to have on the deck of a Royal Navy ship of war.

Alexander reflected that conquest was the way of the world. Ireland had fallen despite its wild nature—Alexander couldn't shake the image from his mind of shaggy-haired Irish Celtic warriors or the great savage wolves that had once roamed the island, terrorizing the survivors of the armada shipwrecks.

Spanish, Normans, Scots, now the French—it seemed at every turn that someone wanted to invade and conquer England. Some had, or nearly had, which made the threat of Napoleon seem so urgent. Given half a chance, the enemy would come storming across the channel. What would be England's fate?

The king would lose his throne and would possibly lose his head. The guillotine might be set up in every English village square. Aristocratic families would lose their lands—even Kingston Hall might be seized and occupied by some Napoleonist. Gryphons would be taken away and forced to fight for the French. The armies and navies would be disbanded or made into mercenaries for Napoleon. Every Englishman would lose his rights—they would be nothing but Bonaparte's slaves. The thought made Alexander shudder.

"Pray tell what is wrong with you, Mr. Hope? You look as if you have just met your own ghost."

Alexander realized he had nearly walked headlong into Captain Amelia, who was busy supervising as a flying harness was put on Desdemona. "Nothing's wrong, ma'am. I was just thinking."

"Haven't you learned by now that thinking will get you into trouble in the Royal Navy?" Amelia turned back to her gryphon. "Come now, Desdemona! Hold still, my girl!"

Amelia's gryphon, long and lean as a greyhound, was antsy to get into the air, shifting from foot to foot and beating her wings, so that the gryphon crew was having a hard time getting all the straps buckled.

Alexander looked up at the blue sky, clear of clouds and with a fresh but gentle breeze blowing. "It's a beautiful day for flying."

"Every day is a beautiful day for flying, Mr. Hope," the gryphon captain remarked. "It just so happens that I'll be leaving you. I'm to go to London to see where I'm needed next. I want to get off this ship while we're still within an easy flight of the coast."

"I am sorry to hear that, Captain," he said. "I had hoped you would be going to Gibraltar with us. I suppose it might be some time before we see you and Desdemona again."

Captain Amelia tugged at a strap. "Now don't go getting teary-eyed on me, Mr. Hope. I have a way of turning up when least expected. Like a bad penny or even a toothache, some might say."

"A toothache?"

"I am being metaphorical, Mr. Hope. Look it up or ask old Hobhouse what that means." She gave him a sidelong look. "Hmm. There is something I've been meaning to say to you. Now seems as good a time as any. I've mentioned it before in passing, but I want you to give my proposal some serious thought. I know you signed on as a navy ensign, but you do have a talent for flying. No fear of heights and barely a teaspoonful of good sense, because what fool volunteers to strap himself onto the back of a flying beastie with claws and a beak that can crack a skull? You're also a bit rash, Mr. Hope. You take crazy chances with your own neck, though you're not half so foolish as Rigley, and thank Jupiter for that. What I'm winding myself up to is that I wondered if you might ever consider a transfer to the Royal Flyer Corps? For the good of the service, mind you."

In reply, Alexander managed to stammer, "That's out of the blue, Captain."

"Like a gryphon, ha, ha! Well, think it over, Mr. Hope. And don't tell Bellingham I've asked you. He won't be happy with me trying to poach his crew. If you tell him I put you up to it, I'll have Desdemona peck your gizzards out."

"With all due respect, last time I believe you were going to have her peck my heart out."

"I've raised the bar, Mr. Hope. Having one's gizzards eaten is far more painful."

Amelia finished checking the various straps and buckles, and then climbed into the saddle.

Without so much as bidding farewell, she flipped the reins and Desdemona leapt over the side, fell for a moment, then spread her wings and caught the sea breeze. In three powerful beats of her wings she was already higher than the mainmast. In another minute Captain Amelia and Desdemona were a mere speck, bound for home. Alexander watched them with a mixture of sadness at seeing them go with excitement over Amelia's suggestion. Become a flyer? It was something to think about.

CHAPTER 16

Captain Bellingham assembled the men, then stood on the quarterdeck to address them. "Today we shall practice our gunnery!" His booming voice was very much like a cannon shot in itself. "Many of the enemy ships are larger than ours and have more guns. Therefore, it is essential that if we should meet them in battle that we fire at a faster rate to even the score. The French shall know that when they meet an English ship, that they have met their match!"

A great swell of voices shouted its approval of the captain's boast.

The captain took out a massive silver pocket watch and held it up so that it glinted in the winter sun. "One minute! That is how much time you will have to load and fire accurately. We will be firing at a raft. Whichever gun crew sinks that raft shall have a gold guinea apiece and roast beef for dinner!"

Another cheer went up. Aboard the *Resolution*, food was always as much of a motivation as gold.

"Lieutenant Swann, let away the raft, if you please." The lieutenant moved to oversee the lowering of the raft, lashed together out of barrels and scrap wood, with a mast flying a pennant on its makeshift deck. "Gun crews to your stations!"

The men swarmed across the deck. It was customary for ensigns to be given command of a section of guns or "division"—Alexander was to oversee three of the guns on the larboard side, on the gun deck below. It was a daunting task, considering that he had never fired a gun before.

Everyone else seemed to know what they were doing, and where they were going. Sailors streamed down the ladders to the gun deck like ants. They had a trick of not using the steps at all, but gripped the outside rail with their feet and slid down. Alexander tried it and landed in a heap, with more sailors getting themselves tangled up with him. Someone grabbed his elbow and pulled him to his feet.

"Come along, young sir. You'll only get trampled there!" He looked up to see Jameson, who then held onto Alexander's coat and dragged him along in his wake as he plowed through the crowd like a bull. Ever since Alexander had risked his own life to save Jameson, the sailor had been extremely loyal to Alexander. It was a breach of etiquette for a sailor to drag an ensign along the gun deck, but Alexander wasn't about to argue.

They moved toward the stern of the ship and came to the last three cannons. "These be our guns, young sir," Jameson announced, and to Alexander's amazement, he tugged his ensign's uniform back into proper order and then stood at attention beside a gun. "Awaiting your command, sir."

All Alexander could do was stare at the cannons. Each barrel was nearly the size of a tree trunk and longer than a man was tall. They were set on a wooden frame or carriage with small wheels at the bottom, so that after the big gun recoiled across the gun deck, it could be rolled back into place to be fired again. These were twelve-pounders—meaning the round shot they fired literally weighed twelve pounds. It was an awful lot of iron moving at incredible speed. The cannonball would punch through the oak sides of an enemy ship, mangle a mast—or certainly sink a floating raft if they were lucky enough to hit the target.

He reached out and touched the massive iron barrel, which felt cold, heavy, and deadly.

Alexander was dumbfounded. Five sailors were assigned to each gun. Here were fifteen men staring at him, waiting for him to tell them what to do. He didn't know what to say. The silence stretched on as the crews around them fell to work.

"Sir?" asked one of the sailors.

"Await my command for the broadside!" shouted Lieutenant Swann, who had overall command of the gun deck. Alexander's men watched him expectantly.

Then Liam was at his side. "The men know what to do," he whispered into Alexander's ear. "Just tell them to make ready."

"Make ready!" Alexander shouted. The three crews sprang into action and took up their positions.

"The rest is easy," Liam whispered. "Load and fire. In between it's your job to aim."

"How am I supposed to aim a cannon?"

"You'll get the hang of it. Just make sure you're not standing right behind the beast when it goes off or it will run you over."

Liam dashed back to his own guns, and Alexander took his advice, shouting, "Load!"

Again, the men had done this many times. A linen sack of gunpowder was brought and rammed down the barrel. Then the cannonball was rolled down the barrel. Liam had told him it was his job to aim, but he had no idea how to do that, and each cannon already had a gun captain who worked a lever to raise or lower the barrel. Alexander was only expected to check their work. Out the gunport he could see the target raft bobbing in the distance.

"Ready?" Lieutenant Swann cried out.

"Ready, sir!" came the replies from the other ensigns, one by one. He heard Roger's voice, and then Liam's.

"Ready, sir!" shouted Alexander. His battery was the last to answer. He felt a lanyard being pressed into his hand by a grinning sailor, who whispered, "To make it go bang, sir." The lanyard pulled the "trigger" on the flintlock mechanism that ignited the power in the barrel, like an oversized musket.

"Fire!" shouted the lieutenant.

Alexander took one last look along the barrel of the cannon, noted where the raft floated, and yanked the lanyard for all he was worth. Someone grabbed him by the collar just as the gun went off, its heavy bulk suddenly occupying the space where Alexander had stood an instant before.

"Beggin' your pardon, young sir," said Jameson, setting him gently back down. "You'll not want to stand directly behind the gun."

His ears rang. The whole ship shook. Geysers of water erupted all around the raft. He couldn't wait to do it again!

He soon discovered that firing a cannon was a

lot like aiming a musket or a fowling piece that had no sights on the barrel. You generally pointed it at what you wanted to hit, sighted along the barrel at the target, and used instinct and experience to aim.

They fired again and again. Each time, Alexander aimed carefully, adjusting the elevation of the barrel based on where their last shot had splashed down. The men seemed somewhat put out that he was taking so long to aim, but it was his theory that each shot should count. Firing blindly wouldn't sink the raft—or teach him the art of aiming a cannon.

He was just lining up the next shot when the raft exploded in a shower of splinters. A great cheer went up from Liam's battery. "Huzzah! Huzzah!"

"Nelson's hat, but they've gone and sunk the raft!" Jameson said. "I thought for sure our next shot would have done for it."

Lieutenant Swann was clapping men on the back. He looked in fine spirits. "I dare say we shall soon have the best gunnery in the fleet. Ha, ha! Now that's what I calling shooting, lads!"

❂   ❂   ❂

The gunnery practice left Alexander feeling exhausted but exhilarated. He didn't mind at all that Liam's gun crew had won the prize. He found himself wishing that instead of a raft in their gun sights that it had been an enemy ship. He said as much to Liam.

"Oh, you'll get your chance soon enough," said the Irish boy, one of the few ensigns who had seen action. "We're not going to Gibraltar on holiday, you know, though half the crew acts like it. It's much easier to fire away at a bunch of barrels lashed together than it is to fire at an enemy ship that's shooting back."

Liam's observation did little to dampen Alexander's spirits. The sailors around him were acting as if they felt the same way, their smiles all the wider and the whites of their eyes that much brighter in faces blackened by the gunpowder and smoke. Even Lieutenant Swann looked quite pleased and swaggered about the gun deck with his chest puffed out. The acrid sulphur smell of burned gunpowder stung the back of Alexander's throat. He truly felt now like part of the crew in a way that he hadn't before. Was this what being in a real sea battle was like, not just an aerial skirmish against enemy gryphons?

He knew he had been given his first real responsibility aboard the *Resolution*—command of a gun battery. The looks of approval—even pride—from Jameson and the other men in the gun crew told Alexander that he had done well.

And yet he found that he could not be

completely happy. Something gnawed at him and he knew at once what it was—Captain Amelia's suggestion that Alexander consider a transfer to become a gryphon flyer. The idea was exciting and he wasn't entirely ready to give it up.

At the same time, even considering a transfer made him feel like a traitor. Captain Bellingham had done him a great favor by taking him aboard *Resolution* as an ensign. Was he willing to be so disloyal as to abandon Bellingham and the *Resolution* in order to take to the air?

Then there was the question of his power—or whatever he might call it. This troubled him most of all. He had seemed so close to having some strange command over water. Maybe it had been in his imagination, thanks to a lucky coincidence or two. He might not be a true elemental at all, but merely one of those not uncommon individuals graced with a few parlor tricks.

He reminded himself that he had rescued Roger and Jameson during the storm—or had he? Some rogue wave may have saved all their lives. It may not have been Alexander's doing at all.

He had tried to save Chloe's little sister when she fell into the mill stream, but had failed. He had not felt so much as a ripple of power. If it had not been for the girls' father, little Celeste would have drowned. Alexander knew he was foolish for even thinking that he could manipulate the water and he hadn't dared to try it since. Whatever power he'd had, he feared that it had abandoned him.

"Some shooting!" Roger shouted in his ear as they splashed at the bucket to wash off the worst of the powder grime. They were all somewhat deaf from the roar of the guns, and their ears rang. "I can't wait to try that on the Napoleonists!"

Dinner in the ensigns' quarters had a festive air, helped by the fact that Fowler was away on watch and that Captain Bellingham had ordered up extra rations for the entire ship. While the guns had been firing, the ship's cooks had been busy roasting beef and baking pies. Alexander crawled into his hammock feeling bone tired, filled to bursting, and happy. And yet his one nagging thought before falling asleep was this: *A flyer? Why not!*

※ ※ ※

Four hours later he was on deck for the midwatch. It was usually dull, cold duty that deprived him of sleep. Tonight the stars were out, the weather was warmer, and the *Resolution* left a phosphorescent wake in the Atlantic. The sight was so strange and beautiful that he almost forgot how much he missed his hammock.

Two saucer-sized yellow eyes stared at him out

of the shadows on deck. Startled, Alexander jumped back. Then he realized just whose eyes those were. "Lemondrop! What are you doing up on deck?"

"He's keeping me company," came a reply, and Lord Parkington materialized to stand beside the gryphon.

"Toby! It's good to see you. Lemondrop must be much better."

"He's almost ready to fly again, praise Jupiter. By that I mean real flying, not the kind we did to escape the French. That was desperate—truth be told, I didn't think he would make it. We can't get back in the air soon enough, as far as I'm concerned. I'm sick of skulking about on deck. I don't know how you sailors stand it!"

"I suppose we manage," Alexander said weakly. He didn't bother to point out that sailors actually worked when on deck. How much longer would he be a sailor? He decided to change the subject. "You picked an unusual time for a stroll on deck. It is the middle of the night, you know. I suppose it's just like a flyer to keep odd hours."

As soon as he said it, Alexander felt a pang. *He* could be a flyer. With Captain Amelia's backing, all he had to do was put in for a transfer.

"The gryphons have been out of sorts all day because of your gunnery practice," his lordship explained. "Actually, there was another reason I came up on deck, Alexander. I had hoped to find you on watch. You see, I came to warn you."

"Warn me about what?"

"I overheard some of the crew talking. It's sailors' gossip, I know, but they said Fowler has it in for you. He's out to get you, Alexander. You had better watch your back. I know I told Fowler that I would have Lemondrop devour him if anything happened to you, but either he's forgotten or he thinks I won't make good on the threat. Fowler is sadly mistaken in that regard, but I'd much rather have Lemondrop eat him *before* something bad happens to you at his hands. The trick is, I don't have an excuse yet."

"Fowler." The name even tasted bad as he said it. Alexander wasn't exactly afraid, but he knew Toby was right—he would have to be on guard. "Thanks for the warning."

"Don't mention it," his lordship said. "It's the least I could do for the sailor who got me out of France."

With that, Lord Parkington and Lemondrop melted back into the shadows. It amazed Alexander that something as big as a gryphon could disappear so quietly. He suddenly felt very alone on deck, and more than a little defenseless. A few weeks ago he might have been afraid and intimidated by Toby's warning about Fowler. Now he was angry—and apprehensive. Fowler was a bully, and desperately close to being a failure in his naval career if he wasn't advanced to lieutenant soon, but he was cunning. Dangerously so. He also had the assistance of his two thuggish cronies, Sweeney and Lloyd. That made it three against one.

On board a ship at sea, it would be terribly easy to arrange for an accident to befall Alexander. It was likely that no one would question it twice if Alexander suffered a nasty tumble from the rigging or apparently slipped and hit his head in the dark of a night watch. Captain Bellingham and the other officers would accept that the fault lay with Alexander's unfamiliarity with the ways of the ship and the sea. Toby was right; he must watch his back.

The marine sentry turned the hourglass and rang the brass bell to mark the time. Alexander stood at the rail and stared glumly at the dark sea. His thoughts were interrupted by the helmsman at the ship's wheel calling his name.

"Ensign Hope, come over here now and let me give you a proper lesson in how to steer the ship."

"All right, then." He moved to stand beside the helmsman, a salty older sailor named Cullins, who had his long hair in a gray queue down his back and a cutlass scar across one cheek. Alexander asked uncertainly, "You want me to steer?"

"Aye, lad, and who better to teach you than ol' Cullins, eh? I done sailed ships through tempests with the waves so big they had to lash me to the wheel to keep from washing overboard. Now, go ahead and take the wheel. Go on now. Get a good grip. That's eight hundred ton of frigate in your hands."

Alexander took the wheel. The wood felt polished and smooth from many hands. It felt natural in his grip. Overhead, wind filled the sails as the stars shined down. "Ah," he managed to say.

"Turn her a bit to port," Cullins directed. "Feel how she responds? Aye, I see from your face that ye do. That's the compass there and we follow the course set by the captain. South south west. There's just enough light from the lantern here to read it. On a clear night such as this a true sailor can navigate by the stars."

Then something curious happened. Through the wheel, Alexander seemed to sense the whole ship in his hands—the canvas sails gently straining, the wooden hull slipping through the water, the rudder creaking as it kept the ship on course. Most of all he felt the sea surrounding them, like something alive.

Cullins laughed gently. "Oh, I see that you have the feel of her already, Mr. Hope. Ha, ha! Maybe you have saltwater in your veins after all, like some on board be saying."

The sigh of the wind in the rigging and the gurgle of the bow cutting the sea was like a song. His heart soared. He realized now how much the idea of becoming a flyer had eaten at him, like a rip current just beneath the surface. Something about it hadn't felt right. *This* felt right. With Alexander at the wheel, *Resolution* sailed toward dawn.

❊ ❊ ❊

In the morning, they had a chance to exercise the guns again. Only this time, it wasn't for practice. After manning the wheel for most of the night under old Cullins's watchful eye, it seemed to Alexander as if he had only just crawled into his hammock when he was awakened by shouts and drumbeats.

"Beat to quarters!" registered dimly in Alexander's sleep-fogged mind. Then he heard someone shout, "Sail ahoy!"

Sighting another sail in the open sea often meant danger. The other ship might be French or Spanish—both dangerous enemies. But this morning, luck was on their side. Captain Bellingham stood on the quarterdeck, studying the distant ship through a long brass telescope. When he lowered the telescope, he was smiling.

"A Spanish merchant sloop, not a navy vessel," he announced. Then Bellingham's powerful voice boomed out, "All hands make sail!"

Dozens of men swarmed into the rigging. Yet

more canvas soon billowed overhead and the *Resolution* surged forward. The merchant sloop had spotted them as well and was making a run for it. The chase was on.

"Will they get away?" Alexander asked anxiously, hardly realizing he was speaking out loud.

"Not a chance of it, young sir," answered Jameson, who happened to be standing nearby. "The *Resolution* is an awful fast frigate when she sets her mind to it."

In time of war, it was customary for Royal Navy ships to capture enemy merchant ships. This was known as taking a prize. The practice had a double benefit. One was that it denied the enemy of ships and supplies. The other benefit was experienced directly by the crew and officers in that captured ships and their cargo were taken into the nearest British-held port and sold for a profit. This was done by sending a small crew to sail the ship. A lucky captain and crew could grow rich from these spoils of war. In a single day, it might be possible to earn a lifetime's wages if the captured vessel held some precious cargo.

An enemy man o' war or privateer would do the same to any English vessels. By gentlemen's agreement, the crew of a ship that surrendered was treated fairly—not invited to dinner but not forced to walk the plank, as pirates might do. The objective was to capture a merchant ship, rather than sink it.

Jameson was right. The chase lasted no more than ten minutes before the Spanish sloop seemed much closer. The little Spanish sloop had not been able to outrun the frigate. They came close enough to finally read the name *Honora* on the stern.

"I do believe we shall scoop her up," Bellingham said. "Mr. Fowler, give the Spaniard a shot across the bow when you have the range."

"Aye, aye, sir."

Fowler ran forward and oversaw the firing of what was called the "bow chaser," a smaller cannon designed for just this purpose. He gave the order to fire and the ball whistled past the sloop to splash into the waves just ahead of her bow. It was clear to all that if she tried to run, she would be blown out of the water. The sloop lowered her sails and waited for the *Resolution* to come alongside. Professor Hobhouse knew Spanish, and he shouted back and forth with the sloop's captain long enough to determine that the ship was heavily laden with a cargo of wine.

"A rich prize, I daresay," said Captain Bellingham. He smiled broadly. "Not bad at all for a morning's work. Hmmm. An ensign's command, I do believe. Mr. Fitzgerald! Take six men and go across to take possession of the sloop. Sail her into the nearest English-held harbor and report back when you can."

"Aye, aye, sir!" Liam grinned from ear to ear, and Alexander was pleased for his friend. Others in the crew touched a knuckle to their foreheads as he passed, which was a traditional sign of respect. Fowler stood at the rail, looking on and scowling. As the senior ensign, he would have been the natural choice to take the prize ship into port, but the captain had chosen a younger boy instead.

"Sometime today if you please, Mr. Fitzgerald!" Bellingham shouted, sounding slightly annoyed. "We are bound for Gibraltar in the king's service, I might remind everyone, and we haven't a moment to lose!"

CHAPTER 17

When Alexander and Roger came off duty a few hours later, they climbed down the ladder to the gun deck, feeling bone weary. The capture of the Spanish sloop had made it an exciting day. The sailors did nothing all afternoon but figure their share of the prize money and how they would spend it in port, which was entertaining, to say the least. There were outlandish schemes that involved everything from buying taverns to starting a zoo. The boys looked forward to a good meal and a long sleep in their hammocks.

"Liam is the captain of his own ship tonight," Roger pointed out. "No sleep for him, or very little. He'll have quite the job running the *Honora* into port under the noses of the enemy."

"Somehow I think our Liam is up to the task," Alexander said. "He's descended from Irish kings, you know."

"Our Liam? Irish kings? Fancy that!" Roger frowned. "There's a lot of bad blood between the Irish and the English. Those Celts are a hot-headed bunch. I hope he remembers whose side he's on."

That thought hadn't crossed Alexander's mind. Then he recalled that Liam *had* seemed a bit put out by King George. He was glad that he hadn't told Roger that Liam also had a bit of Spanish Armada survivor mixed into his family tree, thus making him "Black Irish." That would make him doubly suspicious. Yet Liam was now somewhere on the star-flecked sea tonight, guiding a captured merchant ship into port in the name of King George. He doubted that Liam had failed to notice the irony of that situation.

Alexander sighed. He was too tired to worry much about Liam's complicated family tree or to explain it to Roger. They crossed the gun deck toward the ensigns' berth tucked at one end, and suddenly the only thoughts he had were of food and his hammock. He followed Roger through the doorway.

A large hurricane lantern swung gently to and fro from the overhead beams and lit the narrow room, joined by several beeswax candles. The remains of dinner were still on the table and

Alexander's mouth watered at the sight of a loaf of bread, butter, and a hunk of cold roast beef crusted with salt, pepper and herbs. Several ensigns sat around the table, which was presided over by Fowler, flanked as usual by his two henchmen.

Fowler's eyes flicked immediately to Alexander and he smirked. A flash of silver caught Alexander's attention. He was astonished to see his wristling on Fowler's wrist.

"Pretty, isn't it?" Fowler asked, smiling smugly at Alexander.

"That's mine!"

"I don't know what you're talking about, snotty. I found it lying about."

"Found it in my sea chest, you mean."

Ignoring him, Fowler held the wristling up to the lantern. The woven silver wire glittered in the soft light. "It would be a curious thing for someone who doesn't even own a spare uniform to have," Fowler mused. "Quite valuable, I should think. Quite old. And very mysterious."

"Captain Bellingham gave it to me," Alexander blurted out, wishing instantly that he hadn't said it. He did manage to stop short of adding that the wristling had once been his father's.

"You must be the captain's pet."

"You stole it from my sea chest!"

"Call me a thief, will you?" Fowler nodded at Sweeney and Lloyd. "Bring him here."

Alexander had been so intent on Fowler that he hadn't noticed his two thugs sliding along the wall behind him. They grabbed Alexander and dragged him toward the table. He strained to get up, but Sweeney and Lloyd had arms like oak trees. He glanced at Roger, silently pleading for help, but his friend seemed frozen in place.

Fowler stood up and swept the table clear. The plates and platters clanged to the floor, spilling Alexander's dinner with them. But food was suddenly the furthest thought from his mind as he found himself pinned down on the table, staring up at the low ceiling. He struggled, but Sweeney and Lloyd held him firmly down.

Fowler's face hovered over him. "Captain's pet, eh? We'll see about that." He reached down and yanked up Alexander's shirt, exposing his belly. Then the long dagger Fowler had been toying with the other day was back in his hand. "There's no softer part on your body. I've seen men cut across the belly in a fight and have their guts fall out, like slitting open a sack of eels. They were cut just here."

With the very tip of the knife, Fowler began to etch a red line across Alexander's exposed skin. He did not cut deep, but the sharp point of the knife dragged painfully across Alexander's stomach, leaving a bloody furrow.

Alexander tried hard not to give Fowler the satisfaction, but a gasp of pain escaped his lips.

"Hurts? Well. Tell me, snotty, why would Captain Bellingham give the likes of you a wristling such as this?"

"I'll see you in Hades first," Alexander said through gritted teeth. The scratch on his belly hurt like fire.

"That can be arranged." Fowler slipped on the wristling. It was too big for his wrist and hung loosely. A disappointed looked crossed his face. He took off the wristling and set it on the table. "Pity it doesn't fit. Otherwise I might have kept it. Now, you never answered my question."

He reached for a burning candle.

"Stop it!" cried Roger. "You go too far!"

"The imp speaks," Fowler said.

Roger had seen and heard enough. He was standing next to Lloyd, and gave him a shove. It was enough for Lloyd to loosen his grip on Alexander, who broke free. He snatched the wristling off the table.

"You're going to pay for this, Fowler." He slipped on the wristling, mainly to keep it out of Fowler's clutches. Alexander had never put it on before, but it seemed like the safest place for it at the moment.

"What are you going to do, Mr. Hopeless, blind me with the light sparkling on it?" Fowler laughed. Sweeney and Lloyd already had Roger locked in a strangle hold. Red-faced, he was gasping for breath. Fowler took a step toward

Alexander, twirling the large knife so that it flashed in the lantern light. "Now, let's get back to business, shall we?"

Feeling trapped and defenseless, Alexander backed up against the wall, nearly tripping over the water bucket as he did so. Then a curious thing happened. The cold silver of the wristling grew warm on Alexander's wrist. The wrought wire seemed to shift before his eyes, binding itself to his wrist and expanding until it covered his entire right forearm in a woven silver gauntlet.

A hush had fallen over the room. Then Fowler said, "What in the world?"

Alexander somehow knew just what to do. He dipped his hand into the wooden pail of water on the floor. Instantly, the water changed at his touch, thickening until it wasn't water at all but more like cold, flowing metal. The others stepped back, but Alexander wasn't afraid. He withdrew his hand and found himself holding onto a blue, shimmering whip of liquid ice.

Sweeney and Lloyd stared at him, their eyes round as saucers. They let Roger go.

Fowler snorted. "Snotty, your parlor tricks aren't impressing—"

Alexander didn't let him finish. He flicked the whip at Fowler and wrapped it around the wrist that still held the knife. Alexander yanked and the knife flew out of Fowler's hand. Thrown off balance, the older ensign fell to the floor.

Alexander let the whip uncoil, but when Fowler started to get up, he struck him with the whip with such force that Fowler was thrown into the wall behind him. Shaking his head to clear it, he got to his hands and knees. Then Alexander worked the whip slowly, looping the blue coils around Fowler's throat. He tugged, and Fowler gasped for air like a chained dog, his fingers desperately working to loosen the coils around his neck.

Roger came up next to Alexander and said in a frightened voice, "Let him go, Alexander. You'll kill him. Please."

Reluctantly, Alexander gave the whip a twitch —it was strange, but his hands seemed to know how to work it perfectly—and one by one the coils unwrapped themselves from Fowler's neck. Fowler collapsed onto the floor, panting for breath. Lloyd made a run for the door and Alexander whipped him so hard that he was hurled against Sweeney. Both boys went down in a heap.

Alexander stared at the whip in his hand. The way it glowed seemed to give it a life all its own, like some deep-sea creature. He was suddenly astonished and frightened by what he had done. He dropped the whip. Instantly, it turned back into water and splashed harmlessly to the floor. He started out the door.

"Where are you going?" Roger called.

"I've got to the see the captain!" he replied, running for the ladder.

❂ ❂ ❂

Alexander needed to clear his head. On deck, he stood at the rail and sucked in great lungfuls of sea air. He imagined the oxygen coursing through his body, reaching his fingers, even his toes. His heart pounded less and his head cleared.

The truth was that he had frightened himself.

If Roger hadn't intervened, he realized he may very well have strangled Fowler to death. He had forgotten himself and who he was. The wristling's power had intoxicated him like the strongest wine. He glanced at the wristling. It had shrunk to its old size, but it remained very snug around his wrist. He tugged at it with his left hand, ready to pull the thing off and hurl it into the sea. But it would not budge.

He turned away from the ship's rail and nearly ran into Lieutenant Swann.

"Skylarking on deck, Mr. Hope?"

"Yes, sir. Uh, I mean no, sir."

"Which is it, Mr. Hope?" Ever since the sword-fighting incident, Lieutenant Swann had not been kindly toward him. The lieutenant sighed. "Oh, never mind. Just see that you don't get in the way of anyone who is actually working.

You can do that, Mr. Hope, can't you?"

"Yes, sir."

Lieutenant Swann started to walk away, then stopped. "What is that on your wrist? I don't recall having seen it before."

"Nothing, sir." Alexander tugged his sleeve down. "Just a bauble."

"We don't put much stock in baubles in the Royal Navy. Sailors might wear earrings like a proper pirate, but certainly not an officer." Lieutenant Swann made a sound like harrumph, and then finally moved away.

Alexander felt he had nowhere to go and no one to turn to. Running out of the ensigns' mess, he had planned to see the captain. Now he wasn't so sure that was a good idea. Bellingham might not be pleased that he had nearly killed Fowler—again. He certainly couldn't return yet to the ensigns' berth. The *Resolution* sometimes seemed like such a big ship, but at times like this, it felt like the smallest place in the world—nothing more than a crowded, wooden island.

"Alexander?" asked a quiet voice.

He doubled back to see who had spoken, and found Professor Hobhouse looking down at him from the rigging. Alexander had not seen him right away because the professor had climbed several feet into the rigging and was studying the sky through a telescope. He asked the same question as Lieutenant Swann, but in an amused tone: "Skylarking on deck, are you?"

"Yes, I suppose I am."

"I was just about to make coffee," Professor Hobhouse said. "Would you fancy some?"

"I believe I would, sir. Thank you."

Hobhouse climbed down. He was always so surprisingly agile for such a tall, long-limbed man. Alexander followed him below. The professor's room was very small, but Alexander was glad to have a refuge. No one on board but the captain had much space, and only a few like Hobhouse had anything like a room to call his own. The room contained a bunk, a chair that was mostly a bench, and a table. The sloped walls were completely lined with bookshelves. Consequently, the room felt so cramped that when one of them moved, the other person was almost forced to move as well to make room for him. The professor sat on the edge of the bunk and pointed out the chair to Alexander, as if the room held a confusing number of seating options. A samovar was keeping a pot of coffee warm. He poured them both a cup.

"Forgive me for saying so, Alexander, but you seem out of sorts." Hobhouse was technically a civilian and navy habits hadn't completely taken hold, so he still called people by their first names.

"Do I, sir?" Alexander looked away. He wasn't sure how much to tell the professor, but he felt he had to tell someone who might understand.

He held up his wrist and blurted, "It's this. It seems to be a bit, uh, unusual."

"The wristling that Captain Bellingham gave you."

"You know about it?"

"The captain and I are old friends." Hobhouse peered at the wristling over his eyeglasses. He did look a bit like an owl, as some of the ensigns he taught pointed out behind his back. "Well, it looks ordinary enough, as far as wristlings are concerned. It is very nicely wrought, I might add."

"I just now almost killed Thomas Fowler with it!"

"That seems improbable. In case you haven't noticed, Mr. Hope, it is a piece of jewelry."

"Here, I'll show you." Alexander got up from the chair, which forced Professor Hobhouse to shift his own seat slightly, and then went to a jug of water and bowl intended for washing. He poured water into the bowl and put in his hand. He was afraid at first that it would not work again and that he would look like a fool. But as he pulled out his hand, he found that he was holding a blue, shimmering whip.

"Remarkable," said Hobhouse, staring in wonder at the pulsating whip in Alexander's hand. "I always wondered if the stories were true."

Alexander let go of the whip and let it splash

as water back into the basin.

"What stories?" he asked. Magical items were not unheard of, but they had mostly all been destroyed, lost or locked away by order of the king.

"Captain Bellingham told me about the wristling. He even showed it to me to get my opinion of it. Of course, the wristling belonged to your father."

"I know that," Alexander said impatiently. He was a little worried that Professor Hobhouse was building himself up to a lecture.

"The question is, where did your father get it? I suspect that it is a family heirloom of some kind."

"Why is that?"

"In a word, the armada."

"I don't know what you're talking about. First of all, I was too young to really know my father. Second of all, the Spanish Armada was a long time ago."

"Indeed it was. And yet here we are, still talking about it. You see, some events are not soon forgotten. It's true that Sir Francis Drake was a favorite of Queen Elizabeth, so he received the public praise for the armada's defeat. And Drake was famous for having explored the New World. But it was your ancestor who wielded the real power. With an elemental on the side of the English, the King of Spain never would have dared to attempt an invasion by sea. Unfortunately for him, he only discovered your ancestor's real power once it was too late. Algernon Hope sent dozens of Spanish ships to their doom. They say he set out to meet the fleet alone, rowing his own skiff. It is a remarkable story."

"That's why he was a hero," Alexander said. "Everybody knows how he smashed the enemy fleet. He was murdered soon after that by Spanish assassins out of revenge."

"Mmmm," said Hobhouse in that way of his that indicated there was more to the answer you had just given.

"What don't I know?"

The professor was silent for a long time as he gazed intently at the wristling. "Power is a curious thing," he finally said. "It comes in many shapes and forms. There is political power, economic power, military power. Poets and musicians have their own power, the ability to move people with words or music. Think about the power Queen Elizabeth had. Her father was Henry the Eighth, that most ruthless of kings. She wielded political power as the rightful queen. However, the power of a king or queen can be tenuous in a nation wracked by war and under threat of invasion. A hero such as Sir Francis Drake was no threat to her position. He was a lucky sea captain and explorer. Ultimately, his power came from the queen, who lent him ships and gave him command. Now consider Algernon Hope. He rows out in a skiff and single-handedly destroys an entire Spanish fleet by driving it onto the rocky Irish coast. Where does he get his power?"

Alexander thought about that. "Why, from himself. He didn't need the queen's help to destroy the Spanish fleet."

"You think about what that answer means, Alexander. Think about it, and tell me later who sent those assassins. Now, do you think you can wield that thing at will?"

"You try first." Alexander moved to slide the wristling off, but it seemed bonded to his skin.

The professor held up a hand to stop him. "No, never mind trying to take it off. It's not meant for me. Can you do it again?"

This time, Alexander only reached toward the basin. The whip seemed to leap out and meet his hand.

"Remarkable," Hobhouse said, staring at the pulsating blue coil. "I would suggest you keep this ... weapon to yourself as much as possible. There may come a time when you need something up your sleeve, so to speak."

CHAPTER 18

An uneasy truce settled over the ensigns' berth after the incident involving the wristling. Nobody came out and said it, but it was clear to all that both Fowler and Alexander had gone too far—Fowler's actions had been ungentlemanly and Alexander's retaliation had been violent in the extreme.

It was an ugly affair on both sides, but what was done, was done. Apologies were out of the question. The boys kept their feud to themselves and let an air of unfinished business thicken.

Now that Alexander had the wristling, Fowler was reluctant to challenge him openly. But he was still a bully, and Alexander worried about what might happen if Fowler and his thugs caught

Roger alone. Liam might also be in danger once he returned to the *Resolution*. Alexander sighed. It seemed bad enough that they had to worry about the Napoleonists without having to deal with the likes of Fowler.

Fowler, Sweeney and Lloyd kept to themselves at one end of the room. Alexander and Roger claimed the corner where they hung their hammocks. The dining room table was neutral territory, and by unspoken agreement the two factions took turns eating there.

Fortunately, all the boys had the ship's routine to keep them busy and away from each other's throats. They had their watches to serve, lessons with Professor Hobhouse, and gunnery practice once or twice. Since the capture of the little sloop that Liam had sailed away, they had not seen another sail. Alexander kept hoping that Liam would rejoin them soon. He missed his company—and truth be told, he was a good ally against Fowler.

The weather grew steadily warmer as they sailed south toward Gibraltar. The boys seldom needed their cloaks anymore, even on the night watches. The cold and damp of the English channel seeped out of their bones, replaced by the sunshine and warmth of the Spanish coast.

Then came a perfect, sun-kissed day. The wind fell so that the sails hung limp and the ship only glided along with the tide. Captain Bellingham announced that they would all be going swimming. The men cheered.

"It's not so much the swimming that they're excited about," said Lord Parkington, who had come up on deck with Lemondrop to enjoy the sunshine. "It's the fact that swimming means no working. Captain Bellingham has given them a holiday."

"Maybe the captain should have announced that we're all going sinking, considering that most of the men can't swim," Roger pointed out.

Alexander himself was a strong swimmer. Growing up, he had often spent summer days swimming in one of the ponds or lakes around Kingston Hall. Many sailors had never learned to swim. They pointed out that the idea was to stay *out* of the water.

He soon saw Bellingham's solution. A sail was sunk in the water with one side attached to the ship and the other to floating barrels some distance away. The submerged sail formed a pool so that even those who couldn't swim could venture into the water and not find themselves in over their heads.

Whooping with pleasure, the sailors shed their dirty uniforms and were soon splashing in the sea. The braver ones who were strong swimmers even swam some distance from the sail.

The ensigns looked on enviously. It was beneath the dignity of the officers to splash about with the men, but they ranked somewhere in between.

"May we, sir?" Roger finally asked the captain.

"Of course!" Bellingham replied. "What are you waiting for?"

Alexander and Roger tugged off their uniforms and left them in heaps on the deck. The sun felt wonderful on their bare skin.

"Come on, Toby!" Alexander cried. "Let's jump in!"

"You go ahead."

"Can't you swim?"

"Of course I can swim," his lordship snapped in reply. "But I choose not to."

"Suit yourself." Alexander ran and leaped into the water alongside Roger. The water caught in the sail was pleasantly warmed by the sun. Alexander raced Roger across the pool and then they swam together far into the open ocean. Roger was not a graceful swimmer. When they stopped to tread water, he seemed to flail all around him as if fending off a swarm of bees. Somehow, he managed to stay afloat.

"Why didn't Toby come in?" Roger asked, panting and spluttering.

"Too shy, I reckon."

"Must be a lordship thing," Roger said.

A thought came to Alexander. "I'll bet he doesn't know how to swim!"

They noticed Professor Hobhouse at the ship's

rail, nervously waving them back in.

"What's he going on about?" Roger asked, squinting in the professor's direction.

"Maybe he's worried on account of the sharks."

Roger looked frantically around at the open ocean. "Nobody told me there were sharks."

Alexander laughed. "Maybe you'll swim faster now. Race you back!"

They swam back to the crowded waters of the sail. Some sailors floated on their backs, others engaged in splashing battles. Jameson had made a game of seeing how far he could throw his shipmates. He ducked under, then someone stood on his shoulders, and finally he sprang up, launching the other person into the air.

"Want to try, young sir?" he asked Alexander.

"Yes! Let's see how far you can toss me, Jameson!" Alexander soon found himself whooping as he flew through the air to land with an enormous splash.

When he came up for air, sputtering and laughing, the first thing he heard was a cry of, "Messenger coming!"

He looked up to see a single gryphon winging across the empty blue sky toward *Resolution*. As the rider and gryphon flew closer, he recognized a silhouette he would have known anywhere. It was Captain Amelia and Desdemona, along with a stern rider. Could it be Liam?

As Desdemona circled the ship, she made one of the shrill gryphon calls that set Alexander's teeth on edge. Lemondrop shrieked in answer. Alexander climbed up and hurried across the deck, trying not to drip water on the clothes that lay strewn everywhere, as if a laundry barge had exploded.

No sooner had Desdemona settled gracefully to the deck, then he saw that the other rider was indeed Liam. Flyer crews hurried to help them unbuckle their flying harnesses. Captain Amelia scissored her long legs gracefully and jumped down without any help from the crew. Liam climbed down awkwardly, looking shaken and pale.

"Liam! First time on a gryphon?" Alexander asked.

"Yes, and I'm not in any hurry to get back on one anytime soon."

Captain Amelia sniffed. "Just like a sailor to be ungrateful. Next time, you can try swimming back to your ship." She looked Alexander up and down. "Is it often your habit to parade naked about the deck, Mr. Hope?"

Horribly embarrassed, Alexander grabbed at a corner of sail and wrapped it around his waist. "My apologies, Captain," he managed to mumble, feeling himself turn red.

"Oh, belay that, Mr. Hope. I'm a flyer, not a nun. One doesn't serve in the Flyer Corps without seeing a willy or two. It's not like there's much to look at in your case. I daresay the last time I saw such a skinny arse was on a jackrabbit. Bellingham really must feed you more. Speaking of which, where is the old salt? I've been in the air since dawn to deliver messages and return this sea-lubber while you lot have been splashing about and tanning your nobs. Hmmph. Sure as Nelson's hat, but Bellingham owes me dinner."

❂ ❂ ❂

Alexander found himself invited to dine in the captain's cabin for the second time. He suspected Captain Amelia had had a hand in that—she probably wanted to embarrass him some more. Fresh from his swim, he dressed himself in his one and only uniform—which he feared was beginning to show signs of hard use—and reported to dinner. An invitation to dine with the captain wasn't delivered so much with an "if you choose" but with the air of an order about it.

"You again," said Lord Parkington, who was already seated at the table. He said it in an off-hand way, but he could see from the smile playing at the corners of Parkington's lips that he was glad to see him. Or had the flyers been having a good laugh over him down in their quarters with those smelly gryphons?

"Me again," Alexander agreed.

As usual, Lord Parkington was impeccably dressed, with a crisp white shirt and spotless neck scarf, along with a light blue flyer's coat that looked as if it had just been flown in from a London tailor. His tall boots gleamed with a mirror-like finish. Glancing around the table, it was clear that Lord Parkington was the best-dressed person there. Captain Bellingham was imposing as usual, but he was not wearing his best uniform coat. The one he wore was far from shabby, but somewhere in his sea chest was stowed his very best uniform, saved for meetings with admirals and dinners more important than a gathering in his cabin.

Alexander noticed a stain on his own elbow he hadn't seen before and felt that much shabbier. Then he tugged his sleeve down to make certain it covered the wristling, noticing in the process that his shirt sleeve was becoming rather tattered. The only person at the table who was possibly dressed worse was Professor Hobhouse, who wore a threadbare shirt and an old brown coat with long swallowtails that was so obviously out of date it looked as if it had been made in the reign of the previous king. And yet the professor managed to be shabby in a way that was entirely becoming a scholar. *Eccentric* might be an apt description of the professor, he thought.

"There you are, Mr. Hope," Professor

Hobhouse said. "I wanted to warn you against swimming so far from the ship today. I feared that you might be devoured by Carcharodon carcharias. The Great White Shark. They are known to frequent these waters."

Before he could answer, Captain Amelia came in, wearing her tailored flyer's coat with her tight-fitting riding breeches. Alexander tried to think of a word for how she looked, and found himself blushing.

Bellingham nearly jumped to his feet. "Why, Amelia, there you are!"

"Here I am," Amelia agreed.

Captain Bellingham took her hand and kissed it, keeping it grasped for quite a while, it seemed to Alexander. He noticed Lieutenant Swann and Professor Hobhouse exchange a look. This was not how captains typically greeted one another.

"We have been watching the skies for you, Amelia," Bellingham said.

"You are very kind to say that, James."

He saw Hobhouse and Swann exchange another look. Everyone called the gryphon commander Captain Amelia—she was quite famous for it around the fleet. No one ever called the captain of a Royal Navy ship by his first name at the dinner table of his cabin.

Captain Bellingham smiled. "It is my pleasure. And how are things in London?"

"Oh, I should say they were confounding,

deceitful, back-stabbing and expensive. The butcher wanted a guinea for a lamb to feed Desdemona. In other words, London was about the same as always."

"Did you really pay a guinea for a lamb?" Hobhouse couldn't seem to help wondering out loud. It was an outrageous amount.

"Heavens no. I explained that a hungry gryphon wasn't very particular about what it ate —sheep or shopkeeper made little difference— and he came down quickly on his price. It helped that Desdemona had him cornered and happened to be growling at him."

"Ha, ha!" Bellingham laughed with delight. "I should have liked to have seen that!"

"Come down to the gryphon deck later and I shall be happy to corner you, James."

Alexander began to get that uncomfortable feeling he did whenever he saw old people flirting. Toby kicked his foot under the table and muttered, "This is gross."

Fortunately, Lieutenant Swann chose that moment to raise his glass and announce a toast, "To our friends in the Flyer Corps!"

"Here, here!" Bellingham said, and they all drank to that.

Bellingham had saved the seat of honor to his right for Captain Amelia. The adults at the table all drank port that had been liberated from the hold of the captured Spanish sloop, while the boys enjoyed a much watered-down version.

The food soon followed, preventing any further awkward conversations. They began with steaming bowls of creamy crab bisque, then the main course of roast beef crusted with rosemary, pepper, salt and garlic, served with potatoes and carrots roasted in the same pan as the beef, alongside boiled red cabbage dressed with bacon drippings—truly green vegetables being hard to come by on a ship at sea—and all topped off with a rum-raisin pudding served with coffee.

It was all so delicious that hardly anyone spoke until the last raisin had gone down the hatch. Then Captain Bellingham produced a bottle of French brandy—also captured—and poured small measures for the boys, but much more generous ones for the officers.

He raised his glass. "To the king." He took a sip and smacked his lips appreciatively. "At least the Napoleonists manage to do something right."

Captain Amelia took a drink. "Mmm. By Nelson's hat, but that's delicious. I daresay it might even put hair on Ensign Hope's chest." As Alexander choked on his brandy, his sleeve pulled away and the wristling glittered in the candlelight. He tugged his sleeve back up but it was too late—Amelia had seen it. "Is that your father's wristling?"

"Yes." He was surprised that she knew about it.

Captain Amelia raised her glass. "To Arthur Hope. So promising, and yet he threw it all away."

"Amelia," Captain Bellingham cautioned. "You speak of the boy's father."

"Then why shouldn't he know? Your father was a rising star in the Royal Navy. Some say he had power—real power, not trifling parlor room tricks like some circus elemental. He resigned his commission to go off on some adventure in the Americas." She sighed. "Never to be seen again."

"Impetuous," Lieutenant Swann said.

"Some might say he followed his heart." Amelia gave Alexander an appraising look. "I imagine your father was much like your famous ancestor who crushed the Spanish Armada. Destroyed an entire fleet with a wave of his hand. Think of it! But he would not do the queen's bidding and help her exact revenge by counter-attacking the Spanish. He followed his heart."

"Come, Amelia my dear, let us have another toast," Bellingham said.

But the flyer captain was not finished. "You know, I spoke flippantly before about being home. When I was in London, it was in truth a city wrapped in fear. Uncertainty shrouds it like the nighttime fog. We are surrounded by enemies. It is said the Spanish have an earth elemental, and we know the French have not one but two elementals. Napoleon himself commands fire. What power!"

"Our only defense is vigilance and discipline," Lieutenant Swann said, pounding the table for emphasis. No one seemed to hear him as Amelia went on.

"Two hundred years ago, a single Englishman destroyed an entire enemy fleet," Amelia said quietly. "What sort of boy are you, Alexander Hope? Are you your father's son and your famous ancestor's heir, or are you just another rule-following sea-lubber? I may have seen you bare-arsed today, but I have yet to see your soul."

CHAPTER 19

Alexander was up early the next morning because he was expected on deck. This would be his first time as ensign of the watch, which meant he was second in command after Lieutenant Swann. The lieutenant still seemed skeptical about Alexander, but he kept his opinions to himself. Being ensign of the watch meant Alexander had served long enough aboard the *Resolution* to be entrusted to take command if Lieutenant Swann became indisposed.

That seemed unlikely this fine morning, with the smell of coffee and cooking bacon swirling about deck. Alexander's stomach grumbled, but his breakfast would have to wait until after his watch. He made do with a biscuit and a hot mug of coffee laced with milk and sugar that Jameson brought him.

"Can't have our new ensign o' the watch starvin', now can we?" he explained.

The sun was just peeking above the horizon. The weather today promised to be somewhat more hazy, for all around the *Resolution* lay thick banks of fog or "sea smoke" as the old salts liked to call it. The fog rolled in and out on the light breeze, revealing patches of sunshine and open water.

"I'm going below to talk to the captain, but I shan't be long. Take the glass, Mr. Hope, and keep a sharp lookout," said Lieutenant Swann, handing Alexander his long brass telescope. "A day like this plays tricks with the eyes. Whatever you do, don't cry mermaid and make the hands interrupt their breakfast running to battle stations. They won't thank you for it."

"Cry mermaid, sir?"

"It's the same as crying wolf on land, you see. Haven't you read your Aesop's Fables?"

"Aye, aye, sir."

Lieutenant Swann gave Alexander another one of his searching, narrow-eyed looks that indicated he wasn't quite sure about Mr. Hope, and then moved off toward the ladder that led below.

Alexander did as he was told and kept his eyes on the sea around them. Captain Bellingham had warned that they were now in dangerous waters that swarmed with Napoleonists. The trouble was that the shifting fog, backlit by the rising sun, swirled together at times to resemble an enemy ship. Or so it seemed to Alexander's eyes. Then the next moment what he had thought was a ship evaporated in the shifting breeze.

Old Cullins called out from where he manned the wheel. "This sea smoke is worse than a storm, young sir. You know that a storm is wind and rain and waves." He chuckled in a way that made Alexander wonder if the old man was a bit daft. "Aye, but what does the fog conceal? It deceives the eyes, does the fog."

Alexander tried to ignore Old Cullins and studied the fog all around them. The minutes passed and the sun rose higher. Lieutenant Swann had not returned. *There*. Was that a sail? He put the glass to his eye. Where had it gone? He screwed his eye tightly against the telescope, but all he could see now was a wall of gray. Had his eyes been playing tricks on him again? No, this was not the same. There had been something tangible about that sail.

"Cullins, I think I saw something."

"Aye, did you now?" Old Cullins seemed quick to laugh, but he was very serious now. "If you saw sea smoke and beat to quarters, the men will just think you a foolish ensign. If it's a Napoleonist ship and she gets the first broadside, she might sink us. Which would you say is worse, young sir?

But I can't tell you what to do, seeing as to how you be the ensign of the watch."

Alexander knew what he had seen. "Beat to quarters!" he shouted.

At Alexander's command, the marine drummer on duty pounded out the alarm. Shouts of "Beat to quarters!" echoed across the ship. Below decks, the *Resolutions* abandoned their breakfasts and swarmed up the ladders. Guns were unlashed and run out. Marine snipers climbed into the rigging. The surgeon set out his bandages, flensing knives and bone saws.

In less than two minutes, the sleepy dawn-touched deck was transformed into a ship ready for battle. Alexander watched nervously as Captain Bellingham appeared on deck, tugging on his coat and looking unhappily at the empty fog all around them. Lieutenant Swann was right behind him.

"What is your report, Mr. Hope?"

Alexander brought himself to attention. "I think I saw a sail, sir."

"You think you saw a sail? Mr. Hope, either you did or you didn't."

"It's this fog, sir," Lieutenant Swann said quietly, so as not to be overhead. "I believe it has played tricks on Mr. Hope's eyes. I shouldn't have an ensign on deck alone—"

Boom. There was no need to explain himself further. Guns roared off to starboard and the fog was punctuated by muzzle flashes.

The men began to shout and point, but Captain Bellingham's powerful voice squelched them. "All quiet on deck! They'll have a devil of a time seeing us, so let's not let them hear us."

The silence was filled by several more deep booms. The shots came close together, but were of a slightly different sound. "What do you make of it, Swann?" the captain asked.

"They aren't firing at us, praise Neptune, or we'd all be treading water already, sir."

"Then who are they firing at, pray tell?"

That was the question on the minds of all the men on deck. Nearly every pair of eyes was peering into the fog toward the sound of the guns. They soon got their answer as the fog shifted, revealing two ships battling on the open sea. The larger ship was clearly a French frigate, flying Napoleon's banner. The ship was every bit as large as the *Resolution*. The French ship was firing at a smaller sloop that flew the British flag. A ripple of indignation ran through the crew when they saw the smaller British ship under attack.

"She's attacking one of ours." Bellingham sounded deeply offended.

Lieutenant Swann had the telescope to his eye. "I can see the name on the stern of the French ship, sir. She's called *Chasseur*. I make her out to be a thirty-eight gun frigate. The sloop likely carries fourteen guns and half as many men. She's terribly outclassed."

"Let's even the odds, shall we? Make sail! Mr. Fowler, ready those forward guns."

Captain Amelia had come on deck. Her hair was astray and her hat was off. "What is it, Bellingham?"

"French ship, from the looks of it."

"I'll go below and get the gryphons ready. You may require aerial support."

Captain Amelia went to harness Desdemona and the other gryphons. The men flew into action. They knew just what to do. Sails were hoisted to catch the thin breeze—the wind was barely enough to move the fog around, but it did push *Resolution* closer to the sea battle. Within two minutes, they were within range. No one on the French ship seemed to notice them. Then the fog rolled back in.

"Curse this sea smoke!" Bellingham roared. "Steady men. We can't fire blind or we might hit our own."

The *Resolution* crept through the fog toward the sound of the guns. The wind suddenly shifted as it will at sea, blowing harder, and scattered the fog.

"There they are!" someone shouted.

The fog had swept aside and the rising sun sparkled on the water. Ahead of the *Resolution* lay the two ships, which suddenly stopped firing as the *Resolution* appeared. As they watched, the British flag over the sloop seemed to tremble for a moment in the breeze, and then it began to come down.

"They're striking their colors!" someone cried out.

"Are they? Indeed," Bellingham said.

It appeared that the sloop had surrendered and taken down its flag. But then another flag was run up and unfurled in the breeze. Alexander gasped along with the rest of the men. It was a French tri-color.

"It's a trap!" Bellingham shouted. "Hades take these Napoleonists!"

And then the sloop that they had rushed in to rescue opened fire. The enemy's broadside was well-aimed. The noise was like a dozen thunderclaps at once. Shots ripped holes in the *Resolution's* sails and tore a chunk out of the mainmast. Flying splinters left several men writhing in agony on the deck. The *Resolution* was coming at the sloop head on. At the wheel, Old Cullins was working desperately to bring the ship around so that their own broadside would face the two French ships.

But the ship did not turn fast enough. Before *Resolution's* guns could be brought to bear, the second Napoleonist ship opened fire. Twice as many shots now struck the *Resolution* so that the ship shuddered with the impact. One of the yardarms was shot away and came crashing down, bringing an avalanche of sail with it. Men were buried under canvas, cordage and broken wood. More shots ripped the length of the deck.

Moving at supersonic speed, the iron cannonballs made a high-pitched whine that made his skin crawl. Alexander felt the wind and heat of one passing between him and the captain. It missed them both but destroyed the stern rail of the quarterdeck. Others were not so lucky. Cannonballs tore off arms, legs, heads. In an instant, the air was filled with screams and the deck was stained with men's blood.

Alexander felt frozen in place, too terrified to move.

Captain Bellingham's hand on his shoulder snapped him back to the present. "Mr. Hope, I need you at your guns. When we come about, fire as they bear. Then have your men fire at will."

"Aye, aye, sir!"

Alexander ran for the ladder leading down to the gun deck, slipping at one point on something he didn't want to think too much about. Below, everything seemed in confusion. Two or three of the enemy's cannonballs punched through the oak sides of *Resolution*, showering the gun deck with deadly shards of wood. A couple of guns had been knocked over by the impact and men struggled to right them—it was a nearly impossible task considering the weight of the cannons. Alexander saw Jameson and ran toward him. The men knew what to do—they were peering anxiously over the barrels of their guns, waiting for the order to fire.

They didn't have to wait long. Up at the wheel, Old Cullins had finally got *Resolution* turned around so that the guns on this side of the ship now pointed at the larger French vessel.

"Fire!" Alexander shouted. The tremendous broadside with all the guns firing at once rocked *Resolution* back on her heels. Looking out through the gun port, he saw with satisfaction that several shots had struck the *Chasseur*. The men cheered and set to work reloading. They were old hands at this and didn't really need Alexander telling them what to do. Mostly, he stayed out of the way.

Their sense of victory was short-lived, however, because the French ship got off another broadside. Shot and shell whistled all around them, but no shots struck the gun deck. They felt the impact as the ship was hit elsewhere. The *Resolution* seemed to tremble. There was an ominous creaking sound from the mainmast, the base of which ran down through the gun deck into the bowels of the ship.

One of the sailors tugged at his elbow. It was almost impossible to hear anything in the noise and confusion, so the man leaned close enough that his whiskers scraped Alexander's ear.

"Beggin' yer pardon, young sir, but the captain wants you on deck."

What could Bellingham want? Roger took command of Alexander's guns as well as his own, and Alexander ran up on deck. He reported to the captain on the quarterdeck.

"There you are," Bellingham said. His face looked drawn and worried, which was unexpected. "Let me explain the situation, Mr. Hope. They have taken us quite by surprise through their trickery. Let it be a lesson for us all. Now, I would expect they shall try to board us shortly. If that should happen, I will work with Lieutenant Swann to repel the enemy. If I am so engaged, I want you to take command."

"Of the guns?"

"Of the ship, Mr. Hope. The other ensigns will be busy elsewhere, but you and Cullins will steer the ship and defend the quarterdeck as necessary. The marines will be at their own work, so pick another man to be stationed here with you—I might suggest Jameson, who is handy in a fight."

"Yes, sir."

Alexander's head was spinning. Command of the ship? It was more than he could have expected. He suspected that circumstances must have been grim for Captain Bellingham to give the order. He ran and got Jameson, telling him to fetch a brace of pistols and a cutlass whilst he was at it.

The enemy ships had drawn closer, but they kept their distance, still wary of *Resolution's* guns and the marine sharpshooters who peppered their decks with musket fire. He looked up and saw that the gryphons had launched and were forming up. Captain Amelia and Desdemona flew about the rigging high overhead. Then Toby and Lemondrop joined her, along with Rigley and Biscuit. With the ship's other gryphons and flyers, they formed a V formation and swept toward the enemy.

But the French also had gryphons. Alexander saw their dark shapes emerging from the smoke and fog. To his surprise, the Napoleonists' gryphons seemed to ignore Captain Amelia's formation and fly right under them, going straight as an arrow for the *Resolution*, winging in tight and low to the waves.

There was a reason the enemy gryphons did not fly higher or engage the British flyers. As they flew closer, Alexander saw that they were heavily laden, carrying four or five men apiece. A gryphon could not fly far or maneuver well with that kind of weight. He soon saw that the enemy intended only to reach the *Resolution*. It was an advance boarding party, meant to gain a hold over *Resolution's* deck.

The enemy gryphons did not land but hovered over the bow, flapping their enormous wings and hanging above *Resolution's* deck just long enough for the French flyers and marines to leap down. The enemy's gryphons did not land. Freed from their burdens, they suddenly swept up into the rigging and lashed at the red-coated marine snipers with their talons and long beaks, all the while keening their frightening battle cries.

The morning sun flashed on the polished metal armor of the French flyers, who shot down the marines with pistols and slashed at them with sabers. Torn from the rigging, the marine sharpshooters fell screaming to the sea. One or two unfortunates landed on the deck with a deadly thud.

"Confound those beasts!" cried Bellingham, snapping off pistol shots at the gryphons. But the gryphons flew too swiftly to make an easy target. Having decimated the marine defenses, the gryphons plunged down and pounced upon the *Resolutions* defending the bow. None of the French boarding party had fallen, and the half dozen or so fighters were now reinforced by the gryphons and their flyers. They quickly occupied the *Resolution's* bow.

Ensign Fowler had charge of the bow guns and he was trying to get them turned to use against the French attackers, but the guns were heavy, awkward things. Alexander was surprised to see Fowler draw his sword and fend off an attacker who tried to interfere. He would have thought Fowler would be the type to skulk off and hide during a real fight. Yet he seemed to be everywhere at once, his sword blade flashing in the rising sun.

Then a movement caught Alexander's eye. He looked up to see Desdemona and Captain Amelia sweeping in to join the fight. They had broken away from the attack on the French to return and defend the *Resolution* from the enemy gryphons. The pair landed on the bow among the Napoleonists. Cut off from any reinforcements, Captain Amelia was set upon from all sides.

"Amelia!" Bellingham cried out in despair. "What in the Seven Seas is she doing!"

Her sword whipped back and forth, beating back the French blades—but there were too many of them. She backed up a step and lost her footing, falling to the deck. An enemy flyer raised his sword to plunge down for a killing stroke and Alexander felt his heart stop.

It would have been Amelia's last moment, but suddenly Desdemona was there, knocking the man down with a swipe of her talons. Still, the French flyers and their gryphons moved in from all sides. Desdemona reared up on her hind legs and slashed at them furiously with her claws and beak.

Alexander turned to look to the captain for help, but Bellingham was gone. Alexander was astonished to see him leaping across the deck as if he were crossing a flooded stream, jumping from an overturned cannon to a barrel to a broken spar. Then he grabbed a dangling rope and swung over the French barricade to land beside Desdemona.

Roaring with battle rage, he fired pistol after pistol into the French attackers at point blank range. Then he swung his cutlass with such power that it knocked his opponent clear off his feet. The captain was a big, powerful man and his face was contorted with fury. One attacker turned and leaped into the sea rather than face the captain. Captain Amelia had regained her footing and was fighting back again with Desdemona beside her.

Then one of the Napoleonists stepped forward with a blunderbuss and fired at Desdemona. The gryphon collapsed onto the deck and lay still. Bellingham ran the man through with his sword, and the fight for the bow was over.

A cheer went up from the men once the enemy's airborne boarding party had been defeated. No sooner had that victory cry died away than someone shouted an urgent warning.

Alexander looked around with the others, toward a bank of fog touched by the rising sun, and was horrified to see the sail of a third Napoleonist ship bearing down upon them.

CHAPTER 20

"It just gets more an' more interestin', don't it?" Old Cullins remarked. "Give me a storm any day over fighting not one, not two, but three ships!"

He spun the wheel to catch the wind and better align *Resolution* to meet this new challenge. The ship stood at least some chance against one Napoleonist frigate and the sloop—if they were lucky. Against a third enemy ship, however, they were almost certainly doomed. Combined, the ships would have more than twice as many guns and could encircle the *Resolution*. As if to emphasize the thought, a bullet sang past Alexander's ear.

He looked toward the bow, where Captain Amelia was bent over Desdemona, stroking the dying gryphon's head. Once or twice, Desdemona made a weak attempt to struggle to her feet as if to join the fight again, but the flyer captain soothed her. Finally, the gryphon shuddered and lay still. All at once, the color seemed to go out of her fur and feathers. The breeze ruffled them but they had a peculiarly lifeless look.

Alexander felt a pang of loss. After all, it had been Desdemona that carried him into France and back again. She had been such a loyal creature and an agile flyer. He could only imagine how Captain Amelia must feel; she would be heartbroken because she had raised Desdemona from a hatchling.

Captain Amelia did not move until Captain Bellingham took her by the elbow and helped her up. All around them lay dead or wounded French and English sailors. One of the enemy gryphons also lay in a heap—the other two had flown off riderless when the last of the French fell.

The rest of the deck was similarly littered with wounded men and broken debris. Alexander was so used to the sight of the orderly, well-scrubbed deck that the current state of affairs was utterly astonishing to see. And yet the fight was far from over.

"Death and dying is a sad business," Old Cullins remarked, though he never stopped working the wheel. "There's going to be more of that before the day is through, mark my words, young sir!"

Captain Bellingham's voice cut through the din as he hailed the quarterdeck. "Bring her about!"

"Aye, aye, Cap'n!"

Cullins had been doing just that, working feverishly to get the ship turned so that the *Resolution's* port broadside would face the oncoming French ship. They had just as many guns as the Napoleonist frigate, but several had been knocked out of commission. Still, a few shots from the *Resolution* would give the French ship something to think about.

The wind was not cooperating. Even though the sailors not engaged in operating guns trimmed and hauled what was left of the sails to catch the breeze, it escaped the *Resolution*. The wind, however, seemed to favor the newly arrived Napoleonist ship. First, the fog lifted and cleared almost in an instant, revealing blue skies and sunshine. It was such a beautiful morning that it seemed incongruous that a battle was being fought and that men—and gryphons—were dying.

The enemy had laid its trap carefully so that the newcomer had the weather gauge—the wind at its back—thus giving the other ship more maneuverability and speed in a fight. While the battered *Resolution* was still trying to work itself around, the Napoleonist ship spun neatly and positioned itself at an angle to the *Resolution* much like the top of a sloping capital letter T, which meant that it could bring all its guns to bear on the British ship.

Alexander saw the first burst of smoke from the gun ports and threw himself flat.

While there is no safe place to be on a ship receiving the full broadside of an enemy frigate, not being upright is a good way to avoid being hit by flying cannonballs and jagged splinters of wood. Whistling metal singed and scorched the air. Yet more sections of *Resolution's* rigging rained down.

Quickly, Alexander jumped to his feet. Several more men were now wounded, and their mates helped them below to the surgery. He heard a moan nearby on the quarterdeck, and was astounded to see Old Cullins slumped over. He ran to help him.

"Take the wheel, lad!" Cullins said. "It's me arm. A piece of shrapnel went right through. I've survived worse, but I cannot steer the ship with one arm. Take the wheel and steer the ship like Old Cullins showed you!"

The ship was now out of control, with the wheel spinning wildly and with such force that when Alexander grabbed it, his arms felt as if they were being wrenched loose. He held on and wrestled the wheel back around, so that the *Resolution* would be in position for a broadside against the Napoleonist ship.

It was a curious thing. With his hands on the wheel, it felt as if he could sense the sea all around him once more, gurgling under the battered oak planks. The water felt agitated and stirred up, as if it could tell that a battle was taking place. He could almost feel some of the old power he had briefly enjoyed. Where had it gone? How could he ever hope to summon it again, if ever? He was sure they could have used some of that power today to even the odds against the Napoleonists.

The sensation of being connected to the sea did not last long. As the *Resolution* finally warped around, the broadside was brought to bear. Faintly, he could hear a voice cry out, "Fire!" Was that Liam? The mighty guns roared, rocking *Resolution* and sending forth a great cloud of smoke to mix with the departing fog.

The broadside had been well aimed. Several shots struck the enemy ship, knocking loose rigging or splintering the wooden sides. A great cheer rose up from below. "Huzzah!"

Alexander spun the wheel, keeping the *Resolution* parallel to the Napoleonist ship. It was a classic battle position. They were now in a race to see which crew could reload and fire its broadsides the fastest, and with the greater accuracy. From now on, each second—and each shot—might decide the outcome of the battle.

All the gunnery practiced that Captain Bellingham had ordered now made sense.

Ship against ship, it would have been a fair fight. But out of the corner of his eye, he could see the other two ships gliding toward them, like wolves to the kill, ready to tear into *Resolution's* unprotected flanks.

"What about them?" Alexander asked Old Cullins, nodding over his shoulder at the other two approaching enemy ships.

The sailing master raised his good arm to point at the sky. "Gryphons!" he exclaimed. "They'll try to hold them off."

Leading the way was Lord Parkington on Lemondrop, so close that Alexander fancied he could see the gryphon's yellow eyes narrowed with battle fury. With an eerie screeching, Lemondrop charged through the rigging of the Napoleonist ship. His lordship's sword flashed in the morning sun as he hacked at the enemy's sharpshooters. Then he spiraled higher and flung open a bag of bomblets to rain down on the enemy's deck.

Right behind him came Rigley on Biscuit. The sight of the furious, massive gryphon swooping down on them with talons outstretched caused two of the sharpshooters to jump for the sea—or maybe they fell after being paralyzed with fear. Then Rigley let loose his own bag of bomblets. The razor-sharp, spiked bomblets—sharp enough to slash sails—caused confusion on the deck below as sailors scrambled for cover. The other ship was now so close that Alexander could hear the bomblets thunk into the deck or ping off a cannon.

The attacking Napoleonist ship veered off course and the smaller sloop beside it had to steer hard to avoid a collision. On the enemy's deck, the French sailors cursed and shook their fists at Lord Parkington and Lemondrop.

Alexander cheered, then took off his hat and waved it. Toby swept low over the water, returned Alexander's wave, and then spun around to run at the Napoleonist ship again. He almost wished he was up there, fighting as Lord Parkington's stern rider. But at the moment he reminded himself that he had other duties, such as steering a Royal Navy frigate in the midst of a sea battle.

The enemy frigate had used her own gryphons to land the boarding party aboard the *Resolution*. At least one had been killed, and most of the others had been wounded, so that the frigate was now almost defenseless against an air attack. But not for long. The newly arrived French ship had a fresh squadron of gryphons. The gryphon port opened and one by one the ship's squadron launched. They swarmed around the mast of their own ship, gathering their forces, and then formed a V-formation to launch a counterattack.

A gryphon fight in mid air is a spectacular

thing to watch. The two formations flew toward each other at impossible speed and then rushed through one another's ranks. From the deck of the *Resolution*, Alexander held his breath as he observed the smoke and flame of pistols firing, then the flash of swords. The gryphons lashed out with their brutal talons. An enemy flyer clutched at his shoulder and slumped in his saddle, prevented from falling by the flying harness that held him in place.

Then the gryphons broke off into individual battles. Biscuit was set upon by a Napoleonist gryphon that was almost as large, but Rigley skillfully dodged the talons. Biscuit surprised his opponent by being so nimble for his size. The flyer and gryphon maneuvered so that Biscuit came up behind the enemy flyer. Rigley then peppered the Napoleonist with shots from the pistols slung in bandoliers across his chest.

Rigley and his stern rider were distracted by the chase. They did not yet see another enemy flyer swooping up from beneath them. Like a rocket, the Napoleonist gryphon flew straight up between Biscuit and the gryphon he was pursuing. Biscuit bucked wildly in surprise and Rigley fought to regain control—but not before the other flyer had managed to turn and fire on them. The enemy fire had a telling effect. Biscuit veered off, favoring one wing.

When gryphons withdrew from battle, it was

customary to let them go. Most would consider it the honorable thing to do, to let a wounded enemy fly off to fight another day. The Napoleonist flyers did not seem willing to follow convention. Though Biscuit was clearly wounded, both enemy flyers went after him. They seemed intent on forcing him to surrender and land on the enemy ship, or perhaps they sought his utter destruction.

"Leave them alone!" Alexander shouted at the skies, and shook his fist at the enemy. Of course, they could not hear him. Rigley was doing his best to keep Biscuit airborne, but the enemy gryphons flew close and cut at them with swords. Thankfully, their pistols seemed to be expended. Biscuit sank lower toward the waves.

All at once, there were Lemondrop and Toby to the rescue, flying head-on at the enemy gryphons and scattering them. It was enough of a diversion for Biscuit to come plodding back toward the *Resolution*.

Now Lemondrop and Lord Parkington were having to fight both enemy gryphons at once. His lordship was more than a match for them. He soared almost straight up, but then as the French began their pursuit, Lemondrop whirled and dropped on them like a stone. Again, the Napoleonist gryphons scattered, but it would not be long before they regrouped and attacked Lemondrop and Toby once more.

The gryphons' attack on the second Napoleonist ship had slowed it down, but it was still sailing steadily toward the *Resolution*, clearly intending to bring its broadside to bear. The smaller sloop had swung around to *Resolution's* stern and was positioning itself to fire. Any ship was most vulnerable at the stern because a lucky shot could rip the length of the ship's interior, wreaking all sorts of havoc.

Ordinarily, the *Resolution* would have worked her way out of danger, but there were two frigates to be dealt with, both intent on delivering their own broadsides with deadly effect.

Roger and then Liam came barreling up the quarterdeck ladder. Behind them were several of the sailors who ordinarily manned the guns below. The men stopped short of the quarterdeck, because only officers were allowed there.

"Our guns are wrecked," Roger said, trying to catch his breath. "That last broadside knocked most of them over. Many of the men are hurt something terrible, and we're taking on water. Lieutenant Swann sent us up here to see what good we could do."

"We'll be boarded, if we don't sink first," remarked Liam. He took out a powder flask and a bag of pistol balls. "Give me your empty pistols and I'll start loading them. We'll be needing them any minute now."

"Give me a brace of them pistols, young sir," said Old Cullins. "I'll die here defending the wheel before I let them Napoleonists take control of her."

Liam wasn't the only one preparing to defend the ship. Soon Captain Bellingham's voice carried above the din: "Prepare to repel boarders!" he shouted. The boatswain began to hand out more pistols, cutlasses and axes to the crew who could still fight.

From the raised quarterdeck, Alexander had a good view of the carnage on deck. Broken and wounded men lay everywhere. Great patches of blood stained the deck. The tangle of broken spars, downed canvas and severed lines made movement around the ship difficult.

Several of the deck guns had been knocked over, but Fowler was still managing to fight a handful of guns, keeping up a steady fire against the oncoming frigates. But it was more of a token defense, because the nearest frigate's broadside would likely finish them.

Bellingham made his way to the quarterdeck, followed by Captain Amelia. The death of Desdemona had grounded her. She would fight on deck alongside the crew.

There was a lull in the attack as the enemy drew closer, so Bellingham used it to address the men. Alexander thought they were a fierce-looking bunch, their faces bloody or darkened with gunpowder, and now they brandished an array of weapons: pikes, axes, swords and pistols. The remaining marines formed up and fixed bayonets.

Professor Hobhouse had been below, helping the surgeon save what wounded they could. Now he, too, appeared on deck and armed himself with a sword. He caught Alexander's eye and nodded. What did he mean by that?

The enemy frigates loomed closer on either side. Huge numbers of the enemy crowded the rail, waving their own weapons and shouting taunts at *les Anglais*.

"We shall hold them as long as we can," Bellingham said. "This quarterdeck shall be our last line of defense and we shall sell our lives dearly. For England and King George!"

Bellingham raised his cutlass, and the ragged band of *Resolutions* cheered.

"Huzzah! Huzzah!"

The sound stirred Alexander's heart. He might be about to die, but he would do so defending his friends, and the ship.

On either side of them, the Napoleonist frigates moved into position for the killing stroke. The enemy sloop had reached the stern.

"What should I do, sir?" Alexander asked.

"Stay the course, Mr. Hope. I leave command of the wheel to you."

The firing had stopped so that there was only

the sound of wind and the lap of waves against the oak belly of the ship. Both sides, Napoleonist and English, seemed to be holding their breath.

A gryphon came flying in under the sagging sails, and the men crouched and raised their weapons until they recognized Lemondrop. The gryphon beat his wings, hovering for a moment as he looked for a clear place to land, and then settled onto the deck. Lord Parkington slipped off and began running toward the quarterdeck.

"Do something, Alexander!" he cried. "You can end this now! I know you can!"

Then the Napoleonist frigate fired. Most of the cannonballs went high, doing yet more damage to the rigging. A few shots swept low over the deck. Alexander struggled with the ship's wheel. When he looked back, he saw that Lord Parkington's crumpled body lay in a clear space on deck, his bright blue uniform torn and bloody.

Beside him, Captain Amelia made an agonized sound. "Oh, he is dead."

Alexander stared at the broken body of his friend. He stepped away from the wheel and the ship moved restlessly in the ocean current.

"The wheel, if you please, Mr. Hope!" Bellingham said quietly. "I know it's hard, but we must stay broadside to them if we are to defend ourselves."

But Alexander barely heard him. He walked to

the center of the quarterdeck and threw out his arms. He had no concept of what he was doing. He seemed to lose all sense of himself.

Something snapped inside him, like a dam giving way. It was as if there had been some anchor holding him down all this time, during all these long weeks at sea, and now the anchor chain was broken. His mind had been set free.

It had taken the sight of Toby's torn body to do that. Emotion surged through him. *Do something, Alexander!* Those had been Toby's last words. *Do something!* He raised his arms and emptied his mind.

Water rushed into the emptiness. The thought of water.

He suddenly sensed the sea all around him, its vast depth and coldness. He felt its every current. Its power.

A shout of rage escaped him. Then those on deck felt a ripple of energy go through them, like a clap of thunder without the sound. The shockwave was so strong that it knocked men down.

The sea began to rise around the wounded ship. Water boiled and frothed. Alexander raised his arms higher, and two great waves rose from the depths of the ocean, rising higher and higher on either side of the *Resolution*. The men on deck dropped their weapons in fear. Old Cullins pulled himself upright and took the wheel as best he could, making the sign of the ancient gods. Under his capable hands, the *Resolution* rode out the ocean's fury as the sea churned around them.

Two solid waves now reached higher than the mainmast, stretching toward the sky, water streaming down the sides in foaming white rivulets. In his mind, Alexander held the water in his hands, felt it running between his fingertips. The water wanted to be let go. He could hear the sea roaring inside his skull.

Then he brought his arms down. The waves smashed upon the Napoleonist ships. The massive weight of the sea crushed the frigates like matchsticks. Like an afterthought, he flung one arm behind him and a wave rose up and capsized the sloop at their stern. The *Resolution* bobbed and shook, but no harm came to her.

And just as suddenly, the sea was calm again. Only a few gentle waves stirred the surface, which was now marked by debris from the wrecked ships and Napoleonist sailors crying out to be saved.

Captain Bellingham turned to Alexander, his eyes wide as both fear and amazement played across his face. "What have you done?" he asked gently.

Alexander tried to answer, but a crushing pain filled his head, and he sank to his knees as a rushing black void swept over him.

❀ End of Book One ❀

BOWS, STERNS AND OTHER NAUTICAL NOTES

The Sea Lord Chronicles takes place on a Royal Navy ship during a fantastical version of the Napoleonic Wars, so it does help to understand some of the nautical terms and history involved.

Bow The front of the ship.

Stern The back of the ship.

Starboard Looking at the bow, the right side of the ship.

Larboard Looking at the bow, the left side of the ship. Today, the left side is generally known at the port side. It's helpful that both "Larboard" and "Left" both start with the letter "L."

Mainmast The tallest, central mast of the ship.

Foremast The mast closest to the bow.

Mizzenmast The mast closest to the stern.

Yard or Yardarm The cross members that are perpendicular to the masts, from which the sails are suspended.

Quarterdeck In The Sea Lord Chronicles this is an important locale. Generally located at the stern, this is the command center of the ship. In some ships such as *Resolution*, the quarterdeck is elevated slightly from the rest of the deck. The wheel, compass, ship's bell and marine sentry are located here. Only officers and certain personel such as the helmsman and marine sentry are allowed on the quarterdeck. In a modern ship (or on Star Trek, for that matter), the quarterdeck has been replaced by the "bridge."

Frigate (rhymes with diggit) A war ship that typically carried 32 guns and was often used for independent cruises.

32-pound gun Cannons are labeled according to

the weight of the cannonball they fire. The bigger the gun, the farther it could fire and the more damage it could do. Loading and firing a cannon was hot, heavy work, and almost as dangerous for the gun crew as for those on the receiving end of the cannonball.

Ensign (pronounced en sin) This is the lowest-ranking officer in our version of the Royal Navy, though in actuality the rank would have been equivalent to midshipman. Ensign is a rank found in the army and in the United States Navy of that era. It was not uncommon for boys to go to sea at age 12 or 14 as junior officers. Typically, officers came from upper class or at least "respectable" families and had to provide their own uniforms and equipment, plus pay for their own food.

Prizes The Royal Navy kept up a tradition that was as old as warfare itself, which was that captured enemy merchant ships and cargo could be sold for a profit. The money was then divided among the crew, with the captain getting the largest share. It was a great motivating factor for the crew and ship's officers could make a tidy sum on a lucky ship.

Mutiny This was a constant danger aboard a ship. The rank-and-file crew members were sometimes so unhappy with conditions on a ship that they would try to seize control. It was the role of the marines to protect the ship and ship's officers from mutineers. Only officers were allowed to carry weapons. Pistols, cutlasses and boarding axes were kept locked away and given to the crew before a battle.

The Spanish Armada In 1588 the King of Spain launched a fleet of galleons loaded with troops to invade and capture England. In our story, the armada was defeated by the sea elemental Algernon Hope, who was later knighted for his heroism.

Napoleon Bonaparte In 1792 the French people overthrew their king and established a republic. Unfortunately, the revolutionaries were vindictive and bloodthirsty. A young general named Napoleon Bonaparte stepped into the leadership vacuum and announced that he would lead the government. He would turn out to be one of history's greatest military geniuses. In this story he is mad with power and ambition, crushing anyone who questions his right to rule, bringing world war to Europe and North America. He plans the invasion of England. He is the despot of his age, seen as an enemy to freedom much like Hitler, Stalin or Osama bin Laden are seen today.

King George III One of England's longest-ruling monarchs, George III was much-loved by the English people. American history often paints an ugly picture of George III because he was king during the American Revolution, but as it turns out he was very pious, loved his wife and family, and led a rather quiet life dedicated to his country. Much of the daily operation of government was left to ministers and members of parliament, who like most politicians were not to be trusted. He was followed on the throne by Queen Victoria.

Napoleonic Wars For a period of 23 years, England, France and many other European nations were at war. (The American War of 1812 is sometimes seen as part of the Napoleonic Wars.) This was an era of tremendous battles on land and sea, the names of which are still well-known today, including Trafalgar, the Nile, and Waterloo.

ABOUT THE AUTHOR

David Healey grew up on a farm, ran cross country in high school and was an Eagle Scout. He has a degree in English from Washington College and a Master of Fine Arts in Creative Writing from the University of Southern Maine. He has worked as a newspaper reporter, a librarian, and as a college professor. Family legend says his great-great-grandfather was a ship captain who drowned in the Irish Sea. He lives with his family in an old house on the Chesapeake Bay waterfront. Visit him online at www.davidhealey.net.

Also by David Healey

Civil War novels
Sharpshooter
Rebel Fever
Rebel Train

Historical thrillers
Winter Sniper
Time Reich

Non-fiction
1812: Rediscovering Chesapeake Bay's Forgotten War
Delmarva Legends and Lore
Great Storms of the Chesapeake